Gingerbread and Ghosts

A Peridale Cafe MYSTERY

AGATHA FROST

ALSO BY AGATHA FROST

The Scarlet Cove Series
Dead in the Water
Castle on the Hill
Stroke of Death

The Peridale Café Series
Pancakes and Corpses
Lemonade and Lies
Doughnuts and Deception
Chocolate Cake and Chaos
Shortbread and Sorrow
Espresso and Evil
Macarons and Mayhem
Fruit Cake and Fear
Birthday Cake and Bodies
Gingerbread and Ghosts
Cupcakes and Casualties

A Peridale Cafe
MYSTERY

Book Ten

CHAPTER 1

Sitting at the dining table in her small cottage as snow slowly drifted past the window, Julia South turned to the next page in the photo album. She smiled down at her mother and father on their wedding day as she slid the delicate photograph out of the plastic sleeve before turning it over. '*Pearl and Brian South – Christmas Eve 1971*'. They had only been eighteen when they married, but they looked as happy as two people in love could be on their wedding day. Her mother had worn a beautiful, simple white dress with a short train and lace sleeves, paired with a bouquet of white chrysanthemums and a veil in her curled dark hair. Standing in the snowy grounds of St. Peter's Church, she was the definition of a beautiful English rose.

Julia slid the picture back into its sleeve before turning to the next page. Pearl smiled up at her again, eight years later and this time from a hospital bed, a small baby with an almost full head of dark hair in her arms. Even in a hospital gown with tired eyes, holding her newly born first daughter, she looked just as beautiful.

She flicked through a couple more pages until she landed on the next hospital picture. This time Julia was six, and it was baby Sue who was in their mother's arms, their father on the other side of the bed, his pink shirt open at the chest, the back of his mullet hairstyle hitting his collar. She smiled to herself as she carefully turned to the next page.

"*Julia?*" Jessie cried from the kitchen. "I need your help! Everything's going *wrong*!"

Julia forced herself out of the chair before placing the book back on the shelf with the rest of her family albums. She knocked back the last mouthful of her peppermint and liquorice tea before walking through to the kitchen. She stopped in her tracks when she saw what Jessie was wearing.

"Is that *my* dress?" Julia asked as she looked up and down the red summer dress hanging off Jessie's slight frame.

"I borrowed it from your room," Jessie said with a wave of her hands before she tucked her unusually straight and tangle-free hair behind her ears. "What am I going to do? *Look* at them! They're not *perfect*!"

Julia looked down at the tray of still hot and undecorated gingerbread men. Some of them were a little misshapen, but they smelt delicious and well spiced. Julia suspected Jessie had taken the recipe from Julia's mother's handwritten recipe book. When she spotted it out of the corner of her eye under a bag of flour, it warmed her heart that the recipes had found their way to a new generation.

"It's about the taste," Julia said, tilting her head as she stared at the gingerbread men. "Once you decorate them, they'll be beautiful."

"They need to be *perfect*!" Jessie cried, her cheeks reddening as she leaned against the kitchen counter. "It's not going to work."

Julia hurried around the counter to rest both hands on Jessie's shoulders. In the two weeks since the letter confirming the date for their first adoption meeting with Jessie's social worker had landed on the doormat, Jessie had been a nervous wreck. Julia's own nerves paled in comparison to Jessie's, who had been compulsively cleaning every inch of the house as though The Queen herself was paying their cottage a royal visit.

"You just need to be yourself," Julia said with a reassuring squeeze. "I'm sure it's just a routine meeting. They'll see how happy you are here, and that's what's most important to them."

"You don't know her like *I* do," Jessie said, her voice strained. "Kim's been my social worker since I was a kid. She *hates* me."

"I don't know how anyone could hate you," Julia said with a wink. "You're lovely."

Jessie rolled her eyes as she shrugged Julia's hands off. She grabbed an already prepared piping bag and started to outline the gingerbread men in white icing. As usual, her tongue poked out of the side of her mouth, but her hands were shaking.

"Relax," Julia said, resting a hand on the piping bag. "Take your time. You've come a long way since that girl who lived on the streets. You couldn't even bake a sponge cake, and in less than a year you've made a tray of gingerbread men on your own." Julia stepped back and watched as Jessie slowed down her piping after taking a deep breath. "What can I do to help? Do you want me to mix up the next colour?"

"Fluff the cushions in the sitting room," Jessie said quickly as she moved onto the next biscuit. "They keep deflating."

Julia stopped herself from objecting and walked through to the sitting room, the intense scent of cinnamon and apple hitting her in the back of her throat from the half a dozen lit candles on the mantelpiece. She blew out three of them before starting on fluffing up the already plump cushions on the couch.

Jessie had polished every surface more than once and had vacuumed twice already that morning. Julia had been banned from entering the sitting room, and Jessie had even requested that Julia go into the village if she needed to use the bathroom, just in case the social worker needed to go.

As she puffed up the cushion on the armchair, she stared at the twinkling lights on the Christmas tree they had decorated together the night before. Christmas had always been a strange time of year for Julia, especially in the years she had lived in her cottage alone after leaving her ex-husband behind in the city. With her mother's birthday being on

Christmas Day, there was always an air of sadness that surrounded her whenever the festive period started; it was when she missed her the most.

This year, however, Julia had been kept so busy with her detective inspector boyfriend, Barker Brown, and Jessie living with her, she had barely noticed Christmas creeping up. It was not until she had woken up that morning and seen the Christmas tree standing proudly in front of the window that her mind had switched to her mother.

"You're not doing it right!" Jessie cried as she hurried into the sitting room with the finished plate of gingerbread men on one of Julia's best plates. "They need to be bigger. Why have you blown out the candles?"

Jessie placed the plate in the centre of the coffee table, which had been cleared of its usual baking magazines and remote controls, and had taken on a glossy shine Julia had never known it could. Jessie relit the candles before grabbing the cushion from Julia to frantically pull at the stuffing inside until it had blown up to twice its original size. She spent almost half a minute arranging it perfectly in the corner of the armchair.

"Should we light a fire?" Jessie asked, her eyes wide as she stared at the dark grate. "It will be inviting, right?"

The candles had sucked most of the oxygen out of the stuffy room, but Julia did not argue. While Jessie worked on re-fluffing the cushions Julia had already done, Julia stocked wood logs in the grate before padding scrunched up newspaper in the gaps. With an extended lighter, she lit the paper and stepped back as the amber fire licked the wood.

"*Mowgli*!" Jessie cried. "*Get off!*"

Mowgli, Julia's grey Maine Coon, who had jumped up onto the sofa arm, scurried across, disrupting Jessie's perfectly aligned cushions. His claws scratched against the wooden floorboards as he skidded into Julia's room to hide under her bed.

"Look at the time!" Jessie said, her hands in her hair. "I haven't even started on the pot of tea."

"Jessie –"

"Don't tell me to calm down!" Jessie cried, her pale cheeks darkening as her eyes, once again, widened. "This is important to me."

Jessie stared into Julia's eyes, her lashes flickering slightly as the reflection of the roaring fire shone in her black pupils. Julia pulled Jessie into a tight hug, and for a moment, all her stresses seemed to melt away, a mutual reminder of why they were going through the adoption process firing up between them. They had been together for ten months now, and they had changed each other's lives in more ways than either of them could express.

"It will all be fine," Julia reminded her again as she stroked the back of Jessie's hair. "You have nothing to worry about."

Jessie nodded as she pulled away, less tense than when she had gone into the hug. For all her brilliant, mature qualities, she was still just a scared seventeen-year-old girl looking for her place in the world.

"Tea," Jessie said, clicking her fingers together.

She hurried off to the kitchen, leaving Julia alone in the sitting room. She turned to the mirror, the warm glow of the fire and candles washing against her pale skin. She did not know how her life had taken this turn, but she wanted the adoption more than she could explain to Jessie through words; it felt like it was what needed to happen. So much had changed since she had taken in Jessie off the streets after catching her stealing cakes from her café, and it felt like the adoption was exactly what they both needed.

As though knowing it was temporarily safe, Mowgli crept into the sitting room, but he immediately darted back under the bed when he heard a knock at the door. Silence fell on the cottage, the apprehension palpable in the cinnamon and apple tinted air.

Julia walked into the hallway as Jessie walked out of the kitchen with Julia's best china teapot and cups on a silver tray, her hands shaking so much, the sound of rattling china filled the silence. They nodded at each other before Jessie hurried into the sitting room, leaving Julia to walk towards the front door, the shadow of Jessie's social worker barely visible through the frosted windowpane. Catching Jessie's anxiety, Julia adjusted her dark curls in the mirror and wondered if she should have put some makeup on. She swallowed deeply as she reminded herself none of that mattered. Taking a final breath, Julia pushed forward a smile before opening the door.

"Oh, dear!" the short woman cried as a stack of files fell from her arms and onto the snow-covered doorstep. "What a day!"

Julia stared down at the social worker, unsure of what she had been expecting, but knowing this was not it. The other social workers she had dealt with since taking in Jessie had been professionally dressed women, usually with ponytails or sharp bobs. Kim Drinkwater had been cut from a different cloth entirely. Her short dark hair had been parted in the middle with what looked like strong gel, and held back at the temples with small butterfly clips that Julia had not seen since the 1990s. She was wearing a bright yellow shirt, which seemed to have been incorrectly buttoned, a lime green cardigan with rolled up sleeves that appeared too long, a calf-length brown suede skirt, and clunky brown moccasins with long tassels on the front. A purple leather satchel looped over her shoulder to complete the look.

She darted down to scoop up the files before snapping up, her red-tinted lips forming into a grin, a healthy amount of that lipstick on her two large front teeth. Her bright blue eyes were intensified by the similarly coloured frosted eye shadow she had applied from lash to brow.

"You must be Julia," she said, her voice sounding like it should belong to a small girl and not a forty-something-year-old woman. "It's so lovely to finally meet the woman who can handle Jessika Rice."

Julia accepted her hand unsurely with a nervous smile, her vocal cords suddenly frozen in place. She stepped aside to let Kim in, who immediately tripped over the doorframe, dropping the files onto Julia's carpet.

"What am I like?" she cried with a girlish giggle. "My dad always said I was born with two left feet."

She scooped up the papers again and crammed them back into the thick file before straightening up and dusting down her skirt. She turned to the mirror and dusted the melting snow from her hair, but she did not bother to check her teeth.

"It's so lovely around here," Kim exclaimed as she plodded down the hallway, her heavy shoes leaving behind snowy footprints. "Like something off a postcard."

Julia hurried after her into the sitting room, where Jessie was sitting on the edge of the armchair, hands in her lap and her back completely stiff. Kim rounded the couch and planted herself in the middle, paying no attention to the perfectly aligned cushions. She dropped the thick file onto the table with a thud, causing the lid of the teapot to rattle. Without asking, she plucked a gingerbread man from the plate.

"Oh, how delicious," she exclaimed through a full mouth as she spat crumbs down her yellow shirt. "Did you make these, Julia? I heard you were an excellent baker from the other girls. I've been on maternity leave for most of the year, and I can't say I've missed dealing with this case. Thickest file we have at the office."

"Jessie made them," Julia said, hovering by the side of the couch, unsure if she should sit or stand. "Tea?"

"Wonderful!" she exclaimed. "Four sugars."

"*Four?*" Julia asked, the number catching in her throat as she poured the black tea into one of the small cups.

"My dad always said I was born with a head full of sweet teeth," she said with another girlish giggle as she reached for a second gingerbread man. "Where is Jessika, anyway? Late, I suppose? Or hiding? Or has she run away again? Honestly, Julia, you must be a saint because –"

Julia cleared her throat, rested a hand on Jessie's shoulder, and jerked her head down. Kim looked up at Julia before drifting down to Jessie with a squint. She unclipped her bag and pulled out a pair of oversized pink glasses, which magnified her eyes to twice the size.

"*Jessika?*" Kim muttered with a disbelieving laugh. "Oh my days! Look at you! You almost look like a woman."

"*Almost,*" Jessie said through gritted teeth and a smile. "It's been a while."

Kim scooped up the cup of tea, slurping it and

spilling it down her front, her eyes trained on Jessie.

"Who would have thought the most difficult child I've ever had the pleasure of working with would end up so well placed," Kim said, reaching out for the file, and picking up another gingerbread man at the same time. "They should give me an award."

Julia squinted down at the social worker and wondered if the six months Jessie had spent homeless on the streets after running away from the last house placement Kim had put her in deserved an award. She almost wanted to mention that it had been Julia who had offered Jessie a home, but she bit her tongue for Jessie's sake.

"Twenty-three placements," Kim said with a chuckle as she flicked through the heavy file. "*Twenty-three*! That's the most I've seen in my twenty years. I honestly never thought the day would come when someone would want to adopt you."

Julia left Jessie's side and took the seat next to Kim. She glanced over Kim's shoulder at the top paper, bright red writing catching her eye. '*Disruptive and fighting with other children again*'.

"Jessie has settled in very well," Julia said, suddenly feeling defensive of Jessie's journey. "She's got a job, and she's at college one day a week."

"I heard," Kim said before biting off the gingerbread man's head. "These really are delicious, Jessika. You should be proud of yourself."

"I should?" Jessie asked, her brow arching, the teenager re-emerging.

"You seem to have grown up," Kim mumbled through the mouthful. "*Finally*. It took you long enough! I heard things were going great here, but I wanted to see it with my own two eyes. I almost fell out of my chair when the request for adoption came through. I had to check there wasn't more than one Jessika Rice in the system, but lo and behold, it *was* you!"

Hearing the word 'adoption' made Julia's stomach flip, and it seemed to do the same to Jessie. Julia reached out and grabbed the plate of gingerbread men, and held it in front of Kim's face.

"So, what do you think our odds of success are?" Julia asked softly, staring into Kim's hungry eyes. "We want to make it official before Jessie's eighteenth birthday in May."

"Oh, it's an almost certainty," she said through another mouthful of a gingerbread man. "I don't want to speak out of turn, but Jessika is an *exceptional* case. We're in the business of finding happy homes for troubled children, and it seems we've done just that here."

Jessie opened her mouth as though to object, but Julia quickly shook her head and pushed the plate closer to Kim.

"Almost a certainty?" Julia echoed. "Just to be clear, you think this will happen?"

"I'm almost sure of it," she said as she plucked the last gingerbread man from the plate. "I'd better not tell the slimming club how naughty I've been today. But yes, considering no complications arise, it should be a simple process. Jessika has already been here for almost a year now, which helps your case tremendously. It's all a lot quicker than it used to be, especially with the older children. It should be cleared up and official in a matter of months. May I use your bathroom? My doctor told me not to drink tea because of my weak bladder, but I can't resist. My dad says I should have been called Kim Drinktea."

Julia nodded towards the bathroom door with a smile. Kim tripped over the hallway rug before locking herself in the bathroom. When they were alone, they both let out sighs of relief.

"She's a character," Julia whispered, a smile spreading across her face. "I didn't think it would be so easy."

"She's *something*," Jessie said with a roll of her eyes. "If I know the system, which I do, nothing is as easy as it seems. They have a habit of pulling rugs from under people's feet at the drop of a hat."

"We should be okay though," Julia said, a frown creasing her brow. "Shouldn't we?"

Before Jessie could reply, the front door opened and Barker walked down the hallway in his cream trench coat, his dark hair peppered with snow.

"Jesus, Jessie," Barker said with a laugh as he dropped his briefcase behind the sofa. "Did you run out of clothes?"

"*B-Barker*," Julia stuttered, looking past him to the bathroom door. "You're home early."

"I've been looking for you," he said, glancing over his shoulder at the bathroom door, the sound of Kim blowing her nose drifting through. "Is someone here? I went to the café, and I was surprised to see Sue running things. She said something about a meeting?"

Before Julia could explain herself, Kim unlocked the bathroom door and stumbled out, wiping her damp hands on the back of her skirt. She looked up at Barker, her eyes lighting up when they landed on his handsome face.

"And *who* do we have here?" she asked,

wrapping a hand around Barker's arm. "Oh, it's been a while since I've felt a man's muscles under my fingertips."

"Barker Brown," he said as he pulled his arm away from Kim's grasp. He politely extended a hand instead. "Nice to meet you."

"Charmed," Kim said, dropping into a curtsy as she accepted Barker's hand. "Kim Drinkwater. Recently single and available to date."

"This is Barker," Julia said, jumping up as he stared imploringly at her. "My boyfriend. He's a detective inspector."

"An *inspector*?" Kim gasped, her bright eyes widening, her lipstick-covered teeth coming out as a grin took over the lower half of her face. "How *masculine*! You never told me you had a boyfriend, Julia."

"It should be in the files," Julia said quickly. "It's not a problem, is it?"

"Not at all," Kim said, crossing her arms as she took Barker in. "Marriage and kids on the cards?"

"Oh," Barker said, his cheeks blushing. "Erm."

"*Men*!" Kim exclaimed with a giggle as she slapped Barker on the chest. "That's how I lost my last one, and I was already pregnant with his baby! Do you go to the gym, Detective Inspector Brown?"

"Not really," he said, darting back as Kim's hand drifted down his chest.

Kim winked at Barker before shaking her head and dusting down her yellow shirt. She looked back at the plate of gingerbread men and seemed disappointed that she had finished them all already.

"I'll get going," she said as she scurried back for her files, tripping over the rug again. "Everything seems fine here."

"That's all?" Jessie cried, jumping up. "You aren't going to inspect, or interview us separately?"

"It was just a routine visit, Jessika," Kim said, pinching her cheek as she passed her. "I'll be back soon to go into more detail. I just wanted to pop in and make sure you hadn't killed the poor woman yet. I'll be in touch."

With her file tucked against her chest, she walked past Barker, winking at him again as she brushed her shoulder against his chest. Julia was sure she saw Kim inhale the scent of his aftershave. With a wave of her hand, she opened the front door, tripped over the doorframe, and dropped her files once more, before scurrying off to her bright yellow Fiat Cinquecento parked behind Julia's aqua blue Ford Anglia.

"Who was *that*?" Barker asked, his eyes full of

shock as he looked down at his arm. "And can we please never invite her around again?"

"She's my social worker," Jessie said as she walked to her bedroom door, fiddling with the back of the baggy dress. "I need to get out of this thing. I feel like it's fusing with my skin."

"That – that was today?" Barker asked, his voice small and confused. "I didn't know."

"It was just an initial visit," Julia said, not realising she had subconsciously kept news of the visit from Barker. "I didn't want to complicate things right away."

Barker nodded, but he did not look like he understood. When Julia had discussed adopting Jessie, Barker had told her he also wanted to be part of the process, but he had yet to ask Jessie if she wanted that too. Julia knew he was nervous, but time was running out before Jessie's birthday, and Julia did not want to let their window of opportunity pass them by.

"Talk to her," Julia said, resting her hand on Barker's arm, instantly pulling away when she realised it was the same place Kim had touched him. "Jessie won't say no. She looks up to you."

Barker looked past Julia, his eyes wide and unsure. Jessie walked out of her bedroom in her usual black hoody and baggy jeans, her hair pulled into a low ponytail. She collapsed into the armchair, swung her legs over the edge, and pulled her phone from her pocket.

"I just came back to grab some lunch," Barker said quietly before hurrying through to the kitchen. "I'm not stopping."

He returned with a jam sandwich, which he finished before walking out of the door again. Julia felt like a fool for not being more open with him.

"Get your shoes on," Julia said to Jessie after grabbing a box of gingerbread men from the kitchen that she had baked that morning. "We should get back to the café. Sue will be losing her marbles behind that counter."

CHAPTER 2

"How did it go?" Sue asked as she untied the large apron from around her giant baby bump. "I thought it would take all day."

"Fine," Jessie said with a shrug as she walked past Sue and into the kitchen.

Julia looked around the quiet café, and then back at Sue, forcing a smile. Sue cast a glance over her shoulder at Jessie as she draped the apron across the counter. She popped her hip, rested her hand on the small of her back, and arched a brow.

"I know *that* smile," Sue whispered, glancing back at Jessie again as she washed her hands in the kitchen sink. "What happened?"

"Nothing," Julia said quickly. "The social worker is a little odd, but she made the right noises."

"So, why are you fake smiling at me?"

Julia forced the smile even more for a moment before letting it drop. She melted into the counter as she let out a heavy sigh.

"I think I've upset Barker," she whispered as the bell above the café door jingled out, signalling an incoming customer. "I didn't tell him about the meeting, and he walked in."

"Oh, bugger!" Sue said, resting her hand on her forehead. "Baby brain! I told him you were having a meeting. Why didn't you tell him?"

"Because he wants to adopt Jessie too, but he hasn't asked her yet," Julia said, suddenly straightening up and smiling again when Jessie walked out of the kitchen and nudged Sue out of the way of the counter. "I'll see you later, okay?"

Sue squinted at Julia for a moment before shrugging and grabbing her jacket from the hook.

On her way to the door, Sue patted Julia discreetly on the shoulder, which she knew was a signal to call her if she needed to talk about it. Julia smiled her thanks, unsure if there was anything to even talk about.

"*Julia*!" Shilpa Patil, the owner of the post office next door, cried as she appeared behind her. "What delicious treats do you have today? My Jayesh is spending all day and night at the village hall since he joined the Peridale Amateur Dramatics Society, and I'm worried the boy isn't eating. I was going to take him something over and not leave until he has finished every last crumb."

"There's a tray of mince pies fresh from this morning," Julia said, tapping on the glass of the display case. "I'll bag some up and come along with you. I need to get them to finalise the gingerbread samples before I bake two hundred for the opening show tomorrow night."

Julia quickly bagged up three mince pies, grabbed the tin of gingerbread she had brought from her cottage, and headed out the door with Shilpa, leaving Jessie in charge of the café.

As they walked across the snow-covered village green, Julia shook herself from her thoughts to take in the beauty of Peridale in winter. Despite the frosty air nipping at her face and hands, she loved the season more than any other, especially when they were treated to fresh dustings of snow every morning.

"It's like something out of a painting," Shilpa said, waving her hand towards the snow-capped St. Peter's Church next to the village hall. "I wish I could paint so I could attempt to capture the beauty, not that I think the best artist in the world could do such a thing."

Julia cast her gaze to the front of the church as they walked through the grounds, suddenly reminded of the picture of her parents' wedding she had looked at earlier that afternoon. She tried to imagine how they would have felt over forty-five years ago, planning their simple village wedding as love-sick teenagers; Julia would have given almost anything to travel back and be a fly-on-the-wall during that time in their lives.

"It really is beautiful," Julia agreed, her fingers tightening around the gingerbread tin as they approached the old village hall, both of them pausing in front of the poster for '*A Festive Murder*', the play the amateur dramatics club was performing in the run-up to Christmas. The poster proudly announced that the opening night and the following four performances had already sold out. "What do you think about all of this?"

"A murder mystery play at Christmas?" Shilpa said, her finger on her chin. "It can't be any worse than that dreadful performance of '*The Nutcracker*' last year. I heard the young new director has really injected some life into the club. Did you know he wrote the play himself?"

"I think I've heard that same line every day for the last month," Julia chuckled as she looked at the cast list, '*Introducing Dorothy South as Darcy Monroe*' in bold at the top. "Who knew my gran was such a keen actress?"

Leaving the poster behind, the two women swapped the cold church grounds for the warmth of the large village hall, which had been transformed into a temporary theatre, just as it always was at this time of year. Julia softly closed the door when she spotted the dress rehearsal taking place on a make-shift stage on the far side of the hall. Shilpa waved at her son, Jayesh, who was in a darkened booth at the side controlling the sound and lighting. He glanced up from under his baseball cap and nodded at her with a strained smile, all the embarrassment of a teenage boy being interrupted by his mother obvious on his face.

"*Footprints*," said Carlton Michaels, the elderly cleaner, who had worked at the village hall since Julia had been a little girl, as he shuffled behind them with a dry mop. "Always footprints in *my* hall."

They both smiled their apologies before creeping to the back row of empty seats. Carlton's mop followed them until they were seated on the end two chairs.

"*You don't love me, Jimmy!*" Dot exclaimed under her spotlight, barely recognisable under a long brown wig. "You're not the man I married!"

"Darcy, please," said Jimmy, who was played by Marcus Miller, a familiar face in the annual Christmas plays. "I haven't changed a day since our wedding day. Won't you say you love me?"

Dot turned away from Marcus and looked out at the invisible audience, a shaky hand over her thin lips. She caught Julia's eyes, but she didn't react. For a moment, Julia thought Dot was really going to burst into tears, until she turned back and fell into Marcus' arms, sobbing wildly on his shoulder.

"She's really good," Shilpa whispered in Julia's ear. "I never knew your gran was an actress."

"Me neither," Julia whispered back, silently impressed by Dot's performance. "She claims the director scouted her at the Riverswick Christmas market when she was complaining about her mulled wine being cold. According to Gran, he liked her '*fire*' and '*passion*'."

Shilpa giggled before they both turned their attention back to the stage. Julia had sat in on a few rehearsals and had caught snippets of the play, but seeing the characters in full costume brought out a new dimension, leaving her quietly optimistic for the review in *The Peridale Post*, which had given last year's '*The Nutcracker*' one star, claiming it was '*an embarrassment to the great village of Peridale*'.

"This part is good," Shilpa said, nudging Julia in the ribs and nodding at the stage. "Jayesh is so talented. Watch this."

As though on cue for his mother's praise, Jayesh fiddled with some buttons and looked at the stage. The lights behind the fake windows in the study set flickered as deafening thunder echoed through the empty hall. Shilpa beamed proudly before sending her son an enthusiastic thumbs-up, which was obviously ignored.

"I haven't seen this part," Julia whispered, her eyes glued on her gran, who was stumbling around the stage like a mad woman. "Is this supposed to happen?"

"*Watch*!" Shilpa said with a bite of her lip. "She's nailed this part *every* time."

A door in the set opened, and another of the company hurried in, landing in her spotlight perfectly. She was a new addition to the cast Julia had not seen before, but she was blonde and pretty, and did not look much older than Julia.

"*Jimmy!*" the woman cried, turning dramatically to Marcus, lacking the subtlety of Dot's performance. "You promised you'd meet me at the clock! What happened? – *Oh*, Darcy. *You're* here."

"Yes, I am," Dot whispered, leaning over a small table, her face cast in shadow. "And I *know* what you two have been doing behind my back, and at Christmas too. Have you no *shame?*"

Dot pulled something from the table, but her hand was intentionally obscured in shadow. She stumbled forward, the object in front of her, holding it down as though it was a lead weight. All of a sudden, the spotlight shifted, and Dot's arms lifted; she was holding a gun.

"*Darcy!*" Marcus cried, his hands in the air. "Let me explain! It's *Christmas*."

"I've had thirty years of explanations," Dot said calmly, venom in her voice. "And I've had *enough!*"

She fired the gun, a spark flew from the end, and

a boom thundered around the hall. The tin of gingerbread men jumped out of Julia's hands, landing on the floor with a loud metallic clatter. One of the biscuits tumbled out and split in half right down the middle. The director, Ross Miller, Marcus' nephew, looked back at them as silence fell on the hall in a moment Julia could tell was intentionally supposed to be quiet so the audience could soak up the drama.

"*Cut*!" he cried, jumping up flamboyantly, a clipboard in his hands. "This is supposed to be a *closed* rehearsal. No *previews*! Take a ten-minute break everyone and try and come back on *form*, please!"

Marcus sat up, suddenly alive, and pulled off the fake black moustache over his top lip. He similarly peeled off the black wig, revealing his bald head, aging him instantly.

"My back can't take this stunt," Marcus called out as he stood up with the younger blonde's help. "How did it look?"

"You fell like an old sack of spuds," Ross called back as he cast another eye at Julia and Shilpa on the back row. "I said, *no previews*!"

"That's my granddaughter," Dot said quickly as she hurried to the steps at the side of the stage.

"She's catering tomorrow's opening evening."

Ross waved his clipboard as he sat back in his chair, letting Dot know he did not care about who the intruders were. Julia quickly replaced the lid on the metal tin and picked up the broken gingerbread man. She looked around for a bin, but Carlton appeared as though out of nowhere, a plastic bag open in his hands. Julia cautiously dropped it in, trying her best to smile at the frail and sullen man who she knew had probably not smiled a day in his life while cleaning the village hall.

"*Crumbs*," he muttered with a roll of his bulging eyes as he shuffled towards his brush and shovel at the side of the room. "Always *crumbs*!"

Shilpa hurried off to the sound and lighting booth with the mince pies, leaving Julia to meet Dot halfway down the central aisle between the rows of seats. Dot pulled off the brown wig, her familiar roller-set grey curls springing into their usual position.

"What did you think?" Dot asked with a beaming grin as she glanced back at the director. "Do you think I did okay?"

"You were wonderful, Gran."

"You really mean that?"

"I honestly do," Julia said, the surprise clear in

her voice. "You've joined a lot of clubs over the years, but I think you might have found one you have a natural talent for. I always knew you had a penchant for drama, but I never knew you were such a natural actress. I almost forgot it was you up there, especially when you were holding that gun."

"It feels quite satisfying to kill Marcus Miller over and over every night."

"Do you know him?"

"Oh, it's nothing," Dot said with a wave of her hand. "Ancient history."

Dot collapsed into the nearest chair, a dreamy smile on her face, the brown wig clasped to her chest. For a moment, she seemed every inch the aspiring starlet, and not Julia's eighty-three-year-old grandmother.

"This was my dream when I was a girl," Dot said as she stared at the empty stage as Jayesh hurried around to reset things with the help of a young red-headed woman, Shilpa right behind trying to feed him a mince pie. "The stage, the lights, the acting, it's all I ever wanted. Did I ever tell you about the time I worked in the theatre?"

"You didn't," Julia said as she took the seat next to her gran. "I don't remember that."

"Oh, I was a young girl back then, dear," Dot

said as she pushed up her stiff curls at the back. "I was sixteen, and it was my first job. My mother never wanted me to work. She thought it was beneath me. She was a formidable woman who thought I should marry young, and marry rich to secure my future. That was never *my* dream. I grew up watching those glorious black and white movies of the 30s and 40s. That was *my* era. I wanted to be a silver screen siren, like Joan Crawford and Bette Davis. I left school and joined a theatre company. I was only working in the cloakroom, but I'd spend every second there. They'd let me sit in on the rehearsals. Oh, it was a *wonderful* time! I'd fill notebooks with reams and reams of my observations, dreaming that I would one day be on that stage auditioning for my part. I worked there for two years, and then I met your grandfather, Albert. The pipes in the bathroom froze over, and he was a plumber back then. Let's just say it was love at first sight, like those black and white stories I adored on the big screen. I had your father when I was nineteen, and I left my dream behind. It became a silly little girlhood notion that I didn't give much thought to, but on quiet nights I'd sometimes think '*what if*'. I never did get my audition."

"Gran, that's so sad," Julia commiserated,

resting her hand on Dot's. "You should have chased your dream."

"I put being a mother first," she said with a satisfied nod, her chin poking up to the ceiling. "That became my job, and I never complained for a moment. Of course, your grandfather died in the early 70s, and I had to get a job. Women weren't educated the same back then. I was at school during the war, and we didn't think we'd live to see another year, never mind the 70s, so I did what any mother did. I worked every job I could in every place that would accept a widowed single mother. Cleaning, cooking, you name it, I did it. Not that I'm complaining about that now. Everything happened for a reason. Your father met your mother, and had you and Sue, and I wouldn't change anything for the world."

"You're getting your chance now," Julia said as she rested her head on her gran's shoulder. "You belong on that stage."

Dot rested her head against Julia's. The two women sat in silence for a moment as they watched Shilpa force a mince pie into her son's hand.

"Dreams are for chasing, Julia," Dot murmured as she rubbed her thumb along the back of Julia's hand. "You're still young. Don't wait around to go after what you want. Life has a funny way of going by in the blink of an eye." Dot slapped Julia's hand before jumping up and cramming the wig back on top of her head. "I'd better go over my lines for the next scene."

"What about the gingerbread tasting?" Julia asked, cracking open the metal tin. "Don't you all want to sample them before I bake?"

"Oh, Julia!" Dot said with a shake of her brown wig. "You're the best baker in Peridale. Everyone will love whatever you bake, and besides, they're going to be too taken aback by my show-stopping performance, aren't they?"

Dot winked at Julia, flicked her fake hair over her shoulder, and strutted back to the stage with a bouncy spring in her elderly feet. Julia felt a little ashamed she had never known acting had been such a dream of her gran's, even though she was sure she could talk to Dot all day every day for the next year and still not hear every fascinating story she had to tell.

Julia watched as Ross, the director, relayed notes from the script to Dot in front of the stage. He was the youngest director of a Christmas play in Peridale history according to village gossip. Despite his boyish looks and a full head of hair, it seemed he had cracked the whip in a way Bertha Bloom had never been able to in her twenty years sitting in the director's chair, before her forced retirement after '*The Nutcracker*' barely sold out any of the shows.

Leaving the rehearsal to continue, Julia headed for the door, once again followed by Carlton's dry mop and grumbling about footprints. She reached for the handle, but was pushed out of the way and beaten to it by a flash of red hair.

"Oh, *dear*!" Julia cried out as she jumped back, clutching her biscuit tin as the young woman she had seen helping Jayesh on stage burst into the snow, tears streaking her pale cheeks.

"Poppy, *wait*!" Jayesh hurried out after her, slipping through the gap in the door before it closed. "We can *fix* this!"

"You're lucky you have a girl," Shilpa said to Julia, huffing and puffing as she caught up, her hands clutching her knees over her blue sari. "Boys are more trouble than they're worth."

"Problem?" Julia asked as she pulled on the door handle for a second time. "She seemed rather upset."

"She stormed out of one of the dressing rooms like that," Shilpa said with a wave of her hand as she straightened up. "I think my Jayesh is quite taken by her. I'll have to keep an eye on that."

Julia laughed as she looped arms with Shilpa. They headed through the softly falling snow and back across the village green. Shilpa headed back into the post office, leaving Julia to head back into the café, which was now completely empty thanks to the snow. She shrugged off her pink pea coat, rolled up the sleeves of her baggy denim shirt, and pulled on her apron.

"Grab a wooden spoon, Jessie," Julia said as she enthusiastically clapped her hands together. "We have two hundred gingerbread men to bake!"

CHAPTER 3

Julia passed another tray of plastic-wrapped gingerbread men from the boot of her vintage car to Jessie, and Barker passed one to Billy, Jessie's boyfriend.

"These look wicked, Miss S," Billy said as he poked at the tight plastic. "Proper real looking."

Jessie and Billy hurried off through the falling snow in the direction of the warm glow coming from the open door of the village hall. Julia caught Barker's eye and they shared an awkward smile as they waited for Jessie and Billy to return. Thanks to Julia's night of gingerbread making and Barker working on his debut crime novel at his typewriter in the dining room, neither of them had spoken about Jessie's social worker visit. Barker opened his mouth, as though the topic was on the tip of his tongue, but Jessie and Billy quickly returned for their next trays.

"I thought we'd be the only ones here this early," Julia said casually as she looked around at the warmly wrapped up residents of Peridale as they made their way from all directions towards the church grounds. "There's quite a buzz in the air."

"There is," Barker said flatly with a nod as he passed Billy another tray.

Julia passed Jessie a tray with a sigh, her breath turning to steam in the icy air. Jessie squinted at Julia as though trying to figure out if there was something wrong, so Julia pushed forward a smile, much like she had with Sue; just like Sue, Jessie did not seem to believe it either.

When they were alone again, Julia turned to Barker and smiled sympathetically at him, hoping it would ease things. He smiled back, but it seemed like more of an automatic reaction than anything else.

"I should explain," Julia started, her eyes darting down to the snow-covered road. "I should have told you."

"I get it," Barker said, sounding less angry than Julia would have expected. "This is important to you, to both of you, and it's important to me too, but you were right. I haven't plucked up the courage to ask Jessie. It's scary because you two have such a good thing going on, and I thought she didn't like me as much, but –"

"That's just Jessie's way," Julia said with a small laugh.

"Exactly," Barker replied, with a grin so natural it warmed Julia's chest despite how cold she was feeling under her scarf and gloves. "I'm going to ask her tonight."

"You are?"

"Life's too short," he said firmly before grabbing Julia's hands in his. "I want us all to be a family. A *real* family. After what happened with my brothers at my birthday party last month, and losing my nephew, it made me realise what's important and real. *This* is important."

Jessie and Billy returned, prompting them to let

go of each other's hands. The two teenagers both smirked as they accepted the final trays before hurrying into the village hall. Julia shut the boot and locked the car.

"Don't wait around to go after what you want," Julia said suddenly, the words coming to her out of nowhere. "That's what Gran said to me yesterday."

"That's almost wise," Barker said with a wink. "Are you sure it came from your gran?"

Julia and Barker joined the steady flow of people walking towards the village hall. As the fresh snow crunched under her feet, she felt a calming sense of relief flooding through her body. For the first time in a while, she was looking forward to Christmas Day, especially since it would be the first she would be spending with her new family.

To Julia's surprise, most of the seats in the village hall had either been filled or claimed with jackets and scarves. Thanks to Dot, the four of them were sitting in the front row on seats with 'RESERVED' signs on them. Julia took off her coat, unravelled her scarf, and tossed her gloves onto her seat. Leaving Barker to look after them, she slipped backstage.

People with headsets and clipboards darted around like flies, panic and chaos thick in the air. In the midst of it all, Julia spotted Dot sitting in front of a vanity mirror, staring at her wigged self in the warm glow of the lights, a strange sense of calm surrounding her. She immediately snapped out of that calm when the flash of Johnny Watson's camera bulb sparked in her face.

"*No photographs!*" Dot cried, holding up her hand. "Do you think Julie Andrews had to deal with this?"

"It's for *The Peridale Post*," Julia's old school friend said with a fiddle of his glasses. "We could get a front page shot here."

"Oh, well, that's a different story," Dot said, suddenly straightening up and tipping her head up to the camera. "Make sure you find my best light, and can you do that smoothing thing on my skin? Darcy Monroe is, after all, twenty years younger than myself, but I think I get away with it."

"Consider it done," Johnny said with a smirk as he looked through the camera lens before snapping multiple pictures of Dot. "Perfect. I think I got one."

He checked the pictures on the small display of his camera before heading off, smiling at Julia as he went. Julia stepped forward and appeared in Dot's mirror. She immediately turned around and grabbed

Julia's hand, her fingers shaking to the touch.

"I'm so glad to see a familiar face," Dot said, her cold fingers clutching Julia's tightly. "Is everyone out there?"

"Sue and Neil couldn't make it," Julia said as she glanced over the script, which had handwritten notes all down the margins. "She's not feeling too well with the pregnancy at the moment."

"I'm not surprised. She's about to drop with twins! I'm surprised she hasn't gone already. Twins are always early. If I wasn't so past it, I'd think the nerves in *my* stomach were a small child squirming around."

"You'll be amazing," Julia said, giving her hand an encouraging squeeze. "It looks like everyone has come out to support you."

"Or throw tomatoes." Dot turned in her chair and picked up the script. "Ross keeps changing the lines. He's brilliant, but like most writers, he's neurotic. He's so particular about everything that leaves our mouths. I wouldn't be surprised if he tweaks the script after every performance."

Dot dropped the script onto the dressing table before pulling a small silver hip flask from her handbag. She unscrewed the cap, took a deep glug, and replaced it as she let out a small burp.

"Dutch courage," she winced through the burn of whatever she had just drunk. "I'm shaking like a leaf. I don't think it would be so bad if I had my own dressing room. I'm the *star* of the show, and yet it's Marcus and Catherine Miller who get the two dressing rooms. Talk about favouritism!"

"Catherine?" Julia asked, the name not ringing a bell.

"Marcus' wife," Dot replied with a dismissive wave of her hand. "Far too young for him, and in it for the money I suspect. She's playing Mandy Smith, the woman having the affair with Jimmy in the play. I daresay it's not much of a stretch for her to pretend to be in love with him. She's been playing that role for the past six months since their wedding."

Before Julia could ask further questions, a young man with a headset appeared and announced that curtain up was in ten minutes. All of the cast and crew started running around even faster, causing Dot to take another swig from her hip flask. Deciding it would be best to leave her gran to go over her lines in peace, Julia turned on her heels with the intention of heading back to her seat. On her way there, she passed the two aforementioned dressing rooms, one with a star saying '*Marcus*' and another saying '*Catherine*'. Catherine's dressing room door was closed, but Marcus' was open. Julia would not have stopped to look through the gap if she had not seen a flash of red hair, which she instantly recognised as belonging to the young woman who had burst out of the village hall the day before.

Julia crept forward and peered through the gap. Marcus, who looked to be in his sixties without the aid of his character's wig and moustache, leaned into the redhead's ear and whispered something. Julia did not need to hear what the old man was saying to the young woman to feel her shudder. He brushed her hair away from her neck, but it was too much for her. She spun around and ran for the door, crying just as she had when she had pushed Julia out of the way the previous day.

"*Poppy*!" he cried after her, anger clear in his reddened face. "Women."

He locked eyes with Julia and frowned before closing the door. Julia stared at his handmade star for a moment, sickened by what she had just witnessed. Marcus, with his bald head and pot belly, seemed to be the same age as her father. Julia turned and looked for the young redhead, but she had already vanished.

"*Julia*!" Shilpa cried as she ran towards her. "Have you seen Jayesh? I wanted to give him some samosas to keep him going through the show."

"I haven't," Julia said, distracted by her search for a flash of red hair amongst the crew running around them. "Sorry."

"I think I'm more nervous than he is," she said with a stilted laugh, resting her hand on her stomach. "I might help myself to one of these samosas."

Leaving Shilpa backstage, Julia slipped back into the front of the hall. With everyone now in their seats, there was an excited chatter rumbling through the crowd of faces. Julia was surprised that even though she recognised a lot of them, there were many she did not, leading her to wonder how far news of the play had spread.

"How is the old battle axe?" Barker whispered to Julia when she took her seat in between him and Jessie. "Ready for her debut?"

"Unusually nervous," Julia whispered back, her eyes desperately searching for the redheaded woman in the crowd. "I think I just saw something really terrible."

"What?" Barker asked, his brows pinching together.

Before Julia could tell him, the lights suddenly dimmed, and Ross marched onto the stage, stopping when he reached the spotlight. In his purple crushed velvet jacket and fluffy cravat, he looked every inch the eccentric director, even if his youthful face gave him away.

"Good evening, ladies and gentlemen," he announced, his voice echoing without the aid of a microphone. "I hope you're all excited to see the play. I'll keep this short and sweet, I just wanted to introduce myself. My name is Ross Miller, and I am the new director of the Peridale Amateur Dramatics Society. After a *dull* period of *mundane* plays, I hope you will all appreciate the work myself and the excellent cast and crew have put into 'A Festive Murder', a play that I wrote myself especially for you fine people. Please, enjoy the evening because I think you're all going to be pleasantly surprised."

Ross bowed before hurrying off the stage. There was a smattering of applause, which intensified when the curtains drew back to reveal the dark stage. Through the darkness, Julia could see Dot sitting at a kitchen table, staring into a glass of something. Light consumed the darkness, illuminating the scene of a small kitchen with a large Christmas tree in the corner. For a moment, Dot glanced out at the full audience, her nerves obvious, but as though she was an actress with decades of experience, she stood up with her glass in her hand to deliver her opening monologue.

"*Christmas*!" she announced, an unexpected grit to her voice as she stared into the distance. "A time for love and family. A time for us to give and receive, and to realise what's important. *Ha*! This Christmas, my life changed forever, and here is the story of how it happened."

Dot stepped back to her seat at the table, the lights and sound signifying a rewind in time. Julia spotted the redheaded young woman run onto the stage to take away the Christmas tree. When the time travelling stopped, Marcus, as Jimmy, marched through the door in the set and kissed Dot on the cheek. Julia shuddered as she thought about what she had seen in Marcus' dressing room.

If any of the cast were nervous, Julia could not tell. She sat through all of the first act, completely engrossed in the relationship of Jimmy and Darcy Monroe. She forgot about Dot and Marcus, and the outside world. She laughed at their happy times, cried at their sad times, and gasped along with the rest of the hall when Darcy walked in on Jimmy in bed with his assistant, Mandy Smith, played by Marcus' real-life blonde wife, Catherine. When the closing curtains signalled the end of the first act,

Julia found herself clapping rapturously along with everyone else.

"*Wow*," Barker whispered as he clapped too. "Your gran is amazing."

"Even *I'm* enjoying it," Jessie said, also clapping. "I've never even seen a play. I thought they were all boring."

Along with the rest of the people in the hall, they made their way to the tables at the sides where Julia's gingerbread men were being handed out with mulled wine. She watched as people took bites of the carefully decorated biscuits, pleased when she saw the usual closing of the eyes as they enjoyed her creation. Julia grabbed a small cardboard cup of mulled wine, but kindly rejected a gingerbread man; after staying up until the early hours of the morning to finish the order, if she never saw another gingerbread man again, it would be too soon.

Johnny walked over, his camera in one hand, a gingerbread man in the other. He snapped a picture of Julia before taking a bite of the biscuit.

"Delicious as always, Julia," he said as he licked the crumbs from his lips. "I don't know how you do it."

He wandered off with his camera again, snapping other people before wandering back towards the stage. Before Julia knew it, a voice boomed over the speaker system announcing that the interval was coming to an end. With her mulled wine in hand, Julia made her way back to her seat.

"They wouldn't give us any wine," Jessie said with a sulk, her arms crossed. "Wanted ID. Idiots."

Julia took another sip of her mulled wine before passing it to Jessie. She took a sip, screwed up her face, and spat it back into the cup.

"Gross," Jessie said as she wiped her mouth on her sleeve. "You can have it back."

Julia stared down into the cup with a chuckle. It had taken years for her to appreciate the taste of wine, and she was sure she had pulled a similar face on her first tasting at Jessie's age. She carefully placed the cup on the floor just in time for the curtains to open again. The set had changed from the kitchen to a study, and the mood of the characters had obviously shifted. It started with Darcy and Mandy arguing. Darcy slapped Mandy, causing the crowd to gasp. The scene suddenly shifted along, and when Darcy and Jimmy were alone in the study, Julia could sense what was coming.

The argument bubbled up, and Julia found herself edging closer to the stage. When Mandy hurried in, and Darcy walked over to the table, she felt everyone in the village hall squinting into the dark.

"What's in her hand?" Barker whispered.

The light shifted, bringing the gun into view. The entire hall gasped, and for a moment, Dot seemed to break character as she looked down at the gun, which up close, looked incredibly heavy in her hands.

"*Darcy!*" Marcus cried as he stared at the gun, just as he had yesterday during the rehearsal. "Let me explain! It's *Christmas*."

"I've had thirty years of explanations," Dot said, her voice shaking as she held the gun. "And I've had *enough!*"

She squeezed the trigger and fired the gun, and as though he had been hit with the force of a car, Marcus flew backwards at the same time as the sound effect. Silence fell on the hall, all eyes glued on the gun. It seemed to go on much longer than in the rehearsal, and the silence only stopped when Dot dropped the gun and stumbled back, her hands clasped against her mouth. Marcus coughed, his body rising up before deflating like a balloon.

"What have you *done?*" Mandy, played by Marcus' wife, Catherine, cried as she ran to his side.

"You've *killed* him!"

When Julia noticed the trickle of blood running down the side of the stage, she suddenly stood up.

"Julia?" Jessie questioned, tugging on her sleeve. "What are you doing?"

Julia turned to her gran, who locked eyes with her. Julia had no idea what happened next in the play, but she was sure it did not include Darcy ripping off her wig and sliding down the bookcase.

"Why are you all just *sitting* there?" Catherine shrieked, breaking the fourth wall as she stared out past the spotlight and into the crowd. "Somebody *do* something!"

More people joined Julia in standing, the chatter suddenly bubbling up, no one quite sure if what was happening was part of the play. When Barker stood up by Julia's side and grabbed her hand, the seriousness of the situation overtook her. Pulling away from Barker, she sprinted for the steps at the side of the stage. At that moment, the spotlight cut out and the curtains started to close. In the dark, Julia stared down at Marcus, the blood on his motionless white shirt far too real to be fake.

"*Gran*," Julia whispered, her voice shaking as she turned around. "What have you done?"

CHAPTER 4

Julia picked Dot up off the ground and dragged her backstage. She forced her into the seat in front of her dressing table and grabbed her arms.

"Gran?" Julia cried, clicking in front of Dot's eyes. "Gran, I need you to look at me."

Dot's hand shakily reached out for the hip flask on the dressing table, but Julia quickly pushed it out of the way; the last thing Dot needed was more alcohol in her system.

"How much of that did you drink?" Julia asked as she firmly shook Dot's shoulders. "*Gran*? Please say something."

"I just killed a man," Dot mumbled, tears welling up along her lashes as she looked down at her twisted fingers. "I just shot a man dead. I – I don't understand."

"Neither do I," Julia said, crouching down so they were eye level in the dark backstage area. "I need you to tell me what happened."

Dot opened her mouth, but before she could attempt to explain herself, two uniformed officers appeared, followed by Barker.

"Ma'am, please step away," one of the officers said to Julia.

"She's my gran," Julia said firmly, not letting go of Dot's shoulders. "You're not taking her anywhere."

"Julia –" Barker started.

"Don't do this," Julia cried, jumping up, her finger extended to Barker. "Don't tell me this is '*just how it is*'. You *know* her. She didn't do this on purpose. She was *acting*. Someone must have switched the gun. It's obvious!"

The officers looked at each other, and then at

Barker, but his eyes were glued on Julia. He tilted his head, his eyes filled with sadness; Julia knew exactly what was coming next.

"Sir, if she doesn't step away, we'll need to arrest her too," the second officer whispered to Barker. "I know she's your —"

To Julia's surprise, Dot shrugged off her hands and stood up, her spine stiff and her lips tight. She pulled off her microphone and dropped the battery pack onto the dressing table with a thud. With the confidence of ten men, she walked over to the officers with her wrists outstretched and her head held high.

"Go easy on me, fellas," Dot said, strength in her voice. "I'm an old woman."

Barker stepped back, his hand pinching between his brows; he could not watch as his officers arrested Dot. Julia opened her mouth to object, to scream that something had gone wrong, but the words all tried to come at once, jamming deep in her throat. She felt like she was in a nightmare.

"Dorothy South," the arresting officer started as he secured the metal handcuffs around her wrists. "You're under arrest for the murder of Marcus Miller."

As he read Dot her rights, her expression did not

falter. She nodded along that she understood while keeping her composure, which almost made it harder to watch. When they were finished, the officers stood on each side of her, their hands clamping around her slender arms.

"I won't put up a fight," she insisted, holding up her cuffed hands. "Let me walk out of here with my dignity."

The two officers stared at Barker for permission, but all he could offer was a shaky nod. They let go of her arms, and instead of leading her out, one stood in front of her and the other behind to let her walk freely. Dot turned to look at Julia, but before their eyes met, Dot stopped herself and dropped her head. She inhaled deeply and then pointed her chin upwards before walking.

"Barker," Julia said, the word catching at the back of her mouth. "Do something!"

"There are over one hundred witnesses out there," Barker said, his own voice shaking. "You *know* there's nothing I can do right now."

Julia forced out a dry laugh before walking right past Barker and around the side of the stage. She watched as Dot walked slowly through the central aisle of the village hall, the onlookers all staring with their mouths wide open; Julia could have heard a pin drop. The officers each took one of the double doors, leaving Dot to walk through them alone.

"This *has* to be a joke," Jessie cried, her anger echoing around the silent hall. "Julia, tell me this is a joke."

Jessie's eyes darted past Julia, causing her to turn around. Barker walked around the side of the stage like a shy schoolboy on his way to the headmaster's office.

"Barker?" Jessie cried as she pointed at the doors. "*Stop this*!"

All eyes turned expectantly to Barker, except Julia's. She stared ahead at Jessie, smiling apologetically. Jessie shook her head and stumbled back into Billy's arms, the chatter in the village hall erupting almost immediately.

"I have a job to do," Barker said, his hand resting heavily on Julia's shoulder. "I'm so sorry."

Julia shrugged his hand away, unable to look at him just as she could not when Dot had been arrested. She knew it was not his fault, but she could not believe how little of a fight he had put up for her grandmother.

A team of officers arrived moments later and began questioning people one by one before clearing them out of the hall. When it was time for Jessie and

Billy to be questioned, they both walked out of the hall hand in hand, leaving the officers behind. Julia held back and blended in with the crew, who were all huddled by Jayesh's booth, the shared shock of the situation keeping them silent.

The curtain suddenly parted at the side. Catherine stumbled out, mascara tears streaking her cheeks. She collapsed onto one of the chairs on the front row, blood on the hem of her dress. Ross followed her out and handed her a tissue from his pocket. She dabbed at her eyes before bursting into painful sounding sobs. It was not long before an officer walked over to talk to the recently widowed actress.

For the first time since she moved the Christmas tree off stage during the first scene of the play, Poppy, the redheaded young woman, wandered towards the rest of the crew in front of Julia, her wide eyes vacant. Jayesh jumped down from his booth and immediately embraced her, but she quickly pushed him away. She whispered something into his ear, he nodded, and then they both walked off together towards the double doors. Thanks to Jessie and Billy's escape, two officers stopped them from leaving until they had been questioned. They doubled back and sat alone on the back row.

It did not take long for the village hall to thin out as the police worked through who was important and who was just another eyewitness with an identical story to the other hundred plus witnesses. The crew members surrounding Julia began to disappear one by one, and her hopes of sticking around for as long as possible so she could look around unnoticed seemed to be less and less likely to happen. The only person who seemed to be going unseen was Carlton Michaels, the elderly cleaner, who was already shuffling along the tables at the sides of the room, sweeping up the gingerbread men crumbs while mumbling and grumbling under his breath.

In the seat Julia had been sat in, an officer was questioning the director and writing down his statement. When the officer snapped her notepad shut and left Ross alone, Julia took the seat next to him, and for a moment, went unnoticed by the shocked director.

"Can I help you?" he asked, his bravado and enthusiasm from earlier notably absent. "Now isn't the time."

"My name is Julia," she said with an outstretched hand. "Julia South. Dot is my grandmother. I was the one who baked the gingerbread men."

Ross turned in his seat and stared at Julia for a moment. He looked down at her hand but did not take it. Instead, he leaned back in his chair and wiped down his face roughly with his hands.

"Listen, lady," he started. "If you're trying to get paid, your timing is laughable. My uncle was just murdered right before my eyes, my opening night was ruined, and my reputation is never going to survive this."

Ross looked across the hall at Catherine, who was sobbing into a tissue while an officer attempted to comfort her.

"I'm sorry about all of the above," Julia said, edging closer to him. "But my gran didn't murder your uncle. Not intentionally, I believe. I need to know about the gun."

"It was just a prop," he said with a shake of his head. "We got it from one of the old prop boxes. It's just a firecracker. It can't fire real bullets."

"Is it possible someone switched the gun?" Julia asked eagerly, making eye contact with Barker across the hall. "Who had access to the props?"

"Why would someone do that?" Ross cried with a strained laugh. "Who did you say you were again?"

Barker left the officer he was talking to, making

a course for Julia across the hall; she knew she did not have long.

"Just answer my question," she whispered darkly. "Could someone have *switched* the gun?"

"I – I think so," he said with an uncertain nod. "We rehearsed earlier today, and it was still the prop. They're not under lock and key. It was just on a table backstage."

"So, in theory, any one of the cast and crew could have done it?"

Ross frowned at Julia, and for a moment, she thought he was about to laugh at her for even daring to suggest that one of them had switched the gun to intentionally kill Marcus, but his expression darkened when Julia did not falter.

"I suppose so," he muttered with a nod. "Why are you asking me all of this?"

Deciding she had heard everything she was going to, Julia left Ross' side to meet Barker halfway. They stood a metre apart in front of the stage, neither of them seeming to know what to say.

"Forensics are on the way," he said. "Julia, you – "

"Can't be here," she said with a nod. "I know."

"I'm sorry, I'm just –"

"Doing your job," she said, dropping her head.

"It was a different story at your birthday party when it was *your* family on the line."

"That was different," Barker muttered, his brows dropping over his eyes. "I can't do this right now. Just know that I love you, Julia, and I know Dot didn't intentionally murder that man. I'm going to do everything in my power to prove that, but it's not going to be easy."

"Promise me you'll get her out," Julia said, looking him deep in the eyes. "Promise me she's not going to spend Christmas in a cell."

Barker opened his mouth as though he was about to, but he stopped himself. He rubbed across the lines on his forehead, only stopping when his phone rang in his pocket.

"I need to take this," he said helplessly as he frowned at his screen. "Please, Julia. You *have* to understand. We'll talk about this later."

Barker pushed the phone against his ear and turned away. At that moment, the doors opened once again, and people in white forensic suits marched in, ordering everyone to vacate the scene. Julia did not argue. She walked out into the snow, leaving behind her coat, gloves, and scarf.

"He can't promise, but I will," she whispered in the direction of the police station across the village as the wind whipped snowflakes in circles around the village green. "I'll figure this out, Gran. I promise."

AGATHA FROST

CHAPTER 5

Saturdays in Julia's café were always busy, but it seemed half of the village having witnessed Dot shooting Marcus Miller and subsequently walking out of the village hall in handcuffs had made the café the place to be this weekend. After scribbling down every single thing she could think of regarding the event, Julia had spent most of the night nervously baking in her cottage's tiny kitchen, meaning she had more than enough cakes and biscuits to go around.

Thanks to Jessie, Julia was not the one answering the gossipers' endless stream of questions, even if she had to hear them all from the kitchen. She had almost decided to keep the café closed, but Jessie mentioning that it might make Dot look even guiltier had compelled Julia to leave the house. After being refused permission to see Dot at the police station, she was almost glad she had something to do other than pacing back and forth at home.

The timer beeped, making Julia jump from reading over the hastily scribbled notes in her ingredients notepad. She was reading over the page she had written about Marcus Miller, but her knowledge of the man was sparse at best, and her online research had not brought up much either. She grabbed a pair of oven gloves and pulled the cinnamon and apple cake from the middle shelf. After poking a skewer stick through the middle, which came out perfectly clean, she tipped the tin upside down onto a cooling rack. It smelled perfect, and just like the candles in her cottage she had taken inspiration from, but she had no idea what she was going to do with the cake; she had no appetite to eat.

Julia peeked through the pink beads and into the

café, not surprised to see every seat full and the line reaching the door; the bell had not stopped ringing all morning. Jessie served so quickly she was able to dodge most questions, but it did not stop people using the café as their gossip hub.

"She's *never* been very nice," Amy Clark, the church organist, exclaimed loudly enough so that Julia could hear. "I *always* knew there was something funny about her."

"I'd like to say I foresaw this one, but I didn't," Evelyn, the eccentric clairvoyant who ran the B&B, replied as she adjusted her icy blue turban. "My third eye has been a little foggy recently. I think it's all this snow."

Julia stepped away from the beads before she jumped in and said something she might regret. It seemed that everyone had accepted Dot as guilty because so many people had seen it with their own eyes, but no one seemed to be asking the one question Julia could not shake; why would Dot want to kill Marcus, and why in a village hall filled with over one hundred people on the night she was living her girlhood dream? Wanting to take her mind off the question she could not answer without speaking to her gran properly, she began glazing the cake in shiny icing, but her mind was far from the task, and it was not until the icing had dried solid that she realised she had done a shoddy job.

The beaded curtains parted, and instead of turning to see Jessie, she was surprised to see Johnny walk in, a copy of *The Peridale Post* clutched in his hand. He smiled sheepishly at her, but she could barely muster the energy to return it.

"I won't ask how you're feeling," he said, taking a step forward, the newspaper held close to his chest. "I've been up all night trying to piece together the information for an article, but even I can't wrap my head around it, so I dread to think what's going on in your head."

"Let's just say I'm a little confused and numb today," Julia said as she leaned against the silver counter in the middle of the kitchen, her eyes glued on the badly iced cake. "Cinnamon and apple cake? I promise it tastes better than it looks."

"I can't stay," Johnny said, taking a small step back. "My editor has sent me on a mission to get some quotes from some of the cast. I just wanted to warn you."

Julia looked down at the newspaper, her heart sinking to the pit of her stomach. She held her hand out, but Johnny seemed reluctant to pass it over.

"What's the headline?" Julia asked, shaking her

hand at Johnny to pass over the paper. "Is it *that* bad?"

"I didn't come up with it," Johnny said as he slapped the paper down on the counter. "You can thank my editor for that. He was quite pleased with himself this morning."

"'*Dotty Old Woman's Forty-Year Revenge Plot*'," Julia read aloud. "I don't understand."

"Dot's connection to Marcus Miller?" Johnny asked, arching a brow as he fiddled awkwardly with his glasses before gripping onto the strap of his canvas messenger bag. "I thought *you* of all people would know."

Julia shook her head as she read the sub-headline. '*Eighty-three-year-old Peridale resident, Dorothy South, known locally as Dot, fatally shot the man who conned her out of thousands, Marcus Miller, forty-three years after his original conviction during bizarre play scene.*'

Julia squinted down at the three photographs that had been chosen. One of them was a picture Johnny had taken of Dot at her dressing table, but not the one of her posing, the one of her putting her hand up to the camera, her scowling face visible behind her bony fingers. She almost did not recognise the woman in the second picture as her gran, so she was surprised to read that it was her in the caption under the picture. She was a lot younger than Julia had ever seen her, her brown hair curled away from her face, reminding Julia of 'Charlie's Angels' star Farrah Fawcett. She looked to be standing on the steps of a court, a piece of paper in her hand, with a sharply dressed lawyer-type man behind her. The third picture was a police mugshot depicting a young man she did not recognise, and was even more shocked to read that it was Marcus Miller.

"I've never heard of any of this," Julia said, placing the paper on the counter. "Where did you get this stuff?"

"It's all public record," Johnny said defensively, taking the paper back and folding it up before stuffing it into his bag. "Not the sort of stuff you'd find online though. It happened in the 70s, but it was all in our village records. It's common practice at the paper to cross-search names in events like these, but even I was shocked to read all of this."

Julia shook her head as she stared at the cake, unsure of what to focus on first.

"Marcus Miller conned my gran forty years ago?" Julia asked as she folded her arms. "How?"

"Some land scam," Johnny said as he checked

his watch. "I didn't understand it much myself. I'm sorry, Julia, but I really need to go. They're making even more cutbacks at the newspaper. I can't afford to annoy the man upstairs. I just didn't want to blindside you with this. There's not a lot I could do."

"I've heard that a lot recently," Julia mumbled as she grabbed her pink pea coat from the hook. "Thanks for the warning, Johnny. I appreciate it."

"Where are you going?"

"To talk to someone who *will* know about this."

***

HANDS TIGHT AROUND THE STEERING wheel, Julia drove as quickly as she dared up the snow-covered winding lane towards Peridale Manor. She let out a sigh of relief when the large building appeared through the white fog of falling snow. She pulled up next to the bright pink Range Rover that belonged to her father's wife, Katie, and ran to the door, her knuckles instantly beating down on the wood. Her father, Brian, answered, her recently born baby brother, Vinnie, resting over his shoulder.

"Julia," he said with a sad smile as he dabbed at what looked like freshly coughed up milk on his black shirt with a cloth. "I was wondering when I'd be seeing you."

He stepped to the side and held open the door for her. After Julia removed her shoes and coat, she followed her father through the kitchen, which for the first time since she had visited, was not spotlessly clean. Baby bottles and clothes cluttered the surfaces, along with dirty plates and cups.

"Hilary's having physio in the sitting room," he explained as he softly patted Vinnie's back. "It's going to be a while until she's ready to get back to work, but we're not rushing her. She's been through enough, although I think we need to hire another cleaner in the meantime. I'd forgotten how much work it was to raise a baby."

Julia thought about the surprise birthday party she had thrown for Barker at the manor a month ago. It had resulted in one of Barker's nephews being murdered, one of his brothers being jailed, another separating from his wife, and the housekeeper being thrown down the stairs and sent into a coma, which it had taken her a full week to come out of, and who was now struggling to walk thanks to the head injury. The whole ordeal already felt like something that had happened in a bad dream.

"She's alive," Julia said uncertainly. "That's the

main thing."

Brian surprised Julia by passing the baby over to her. Vinnie scowled up at her with his tiny wrinkled face, his tongue resting against his bottom lip. She carefully stroked his wispy dark hair, which was sticking up in every direction. Brian cleared some room on the marble island before clearing the stools of piles of ironed and folded baby clothes. The ironing board and iron in front of the double-fronted fridge told Julia her father had likely been too busy to even worry about what was currently happening to his mother.

"Tea?" he asked, already filling the kettle at the sink. "I still have some of your favourite, peppermint and liquorice."

"That would be great," she said, the thought comforting as she stared down at her brother. "He's so big already."

She tickled under his chin, prompting him to clasp one of his tiny hands around her finger. He kicked his legs, his brows moving up and down as though he was confused by any face that didn't belong to his parents.

"You're lucky he's not crying," Brian said as he prepared the two cups. "Screamed the house down last night. Katie's upstairs having a lie down. Poor thing doesn't look like she's slept in weeks. I can't even remember what it feels like to be fully rested."

The talk of sleep caused Julia to let out a long yawn, which baffled her younger brother even more. She did not bother to mention that she had not had any sleep herself.

"Half the village rang our house phone last night to tell us what happened," Brian said as he poured boiled water into the two cups. "I thought it was a joke at first. Kids taking the mickey, you know? When Amy Clark called, I knew it was serious. I couldn't wrap my head around it, until someone mentioned that it was Marcus Miller that she killed. I'm glad I was sitting down at the time, or that would have knocked me right off my feet. I had no idea he was still knocking around the place."

"You know then?" Julia asked as she bounced Vinnie up and down. "You know about what happened forty-three years ago?"

Brian brought the two cups over to the island before sitting across from Julia. He stared down at Vinnie for a moment, the smile only a father could have taking over his lips. As though he did not even realise he was doing it, he looked up at Julia to give her a more melancholy version of the same smile.

"I went to school with the guy," Brian said as he

blew on the hot surface of his black tea. "We're the same age. Never liked him much. We used to go around in the same circles sometimes, but he was always a nasty piece of work. Messed girls around, if you know what I'm saying. Bit of a player. He was charming and good looking, and that's all you needed back then. When we left school, I didn't see much of him until all that vile business with your gran. I wanted to kill him."

"Why didn't anyone tell me?"

"Because it was forty-something years ago," Brian said with a laugh after slurping the hot tea. "I hadn't given it a second thought in almost as many years, and I doubt your gran had either. Ancient history until yesterday."

Julia looked at her tea, and then down at Vinnie. Not wanting to risk spilling the tea on the baby, she decided to wait. As though her father knew what she was thinking, he walked around to scoop him out of her arms. Instead of holding Vinnie himself, he placed him in the Moses basket on a stand next to the counter.

"He's ready for a nap anyway," he explained as he tucked a blanket over Vinnie's tiny body. "It's not the going to sleep that's the problem, it's staying there."

"What happened between them?" Julia urged, eager to know as much as possible. "I need to know everything."

Brian sat back on his stool before scratching the side of his head. He slurped his tea again, clasped his hands together, and leaned in.

"It's been a long time, Julia," he said with a sigh. "The memory gets foggy with age. I think it was 1975. No, 1974 because I remember the police pulling us out of my twenty-first birthday party at The Plough to question your gran about Marcus. You weren't born then, but I was already married to your mother. She couldn't believe your gran fell for it any more than I could. She was always scared of your gran, but I suppose she was vulnerable when it happened."

Julia sipped her tea, frustrated that her father was talking so vaguely, even if it was nice to hear him talking about her mother, especially at this time of year.

"When *what* happened?" Julia prompted. "And *why* was she vulnerable?"

"My dad had just died," Brian said, his eyes glazing over as though it had happened last week. "Albert. Your grandfather. He was only forty. Nasty car accident. He and your gran were driving back from London after seeing a West End show. They'd go once or twice a month to watch what was new. A drunk driver hit them on the motorway, and they flipped over. You wouldn't believe it, but that was about a decade before seatbelts were required by law. Your gran was wearing one, your grandfather wasn't.

"After that, your gran went into a sort of walking coma. She wasn't herself. She couldn't be. I know that feeling too well. I went through it when your mother died. She was vulnerable, not that she would admit that afterwards. Marcus Miller was sniffing around Peridale looking for people to invest in his property scam. He convinced people, mainly women because that's the type of guy he is, to hand over their money to buy a piece of farmland, promising them that when they sold the whole thing in a couple of years, they would all walk away with ten times more than what they put in. He got your gran at the right time. She was worrying herself sick about money. I was trying to help her the best I could, but I was only working at the pub then. Your mum was working in the old bakery on Mulberry Lane. It closed down a long time ago. We tried our best, but at the time I thought I should have tried more so she didn't feel so much pressure. Being recently widowed makes you feel like your world is coming to an end. When Marcus told her she could get rich quick, I suppose it gave her some hope.

"She handed over two thousand pounds, which doesn't sound like a lot today, but that was worth ten times more back then when you take inflation into account. That was the money my father left behind from his life savings. She handed over every penny, but I think she took some comfort in not being the only one. There are about thirty women across the Cotswolds who each own a square metre of useless farmland. As you can guess, it wasn't worth anything. It was marsh, so no one would ever get permission to build anything on it. I think your gran technically still owns it.

"When the police caught up with him, they unravelled dozens of scams. Everything from money laundering to flogging fake designer watches at the market. He got seven years, but he was out in five. I always thought he'd moved away, but I guess he came back."

"He's been in the Christmas plays for as long as I can remember," Julia said, suddenly remembering what her gran had told her during the dress rehearsal. "She hinted that something had happened between them, but she called it *ancient history* too."

"Because it was," he said, casting an eye at

Vinnie as he began to softly snore through his tiny nostrils. "She even made a point of going to the prison the day he was released to shake his hand and prove there were no hard feelings. It was just after you were born. We went along with you in a pram to make sure she didn't kill him then. I think once the grief had cleared, your gran realised how silly she'd been, and she wanted to show that he hadn't affected her. Your gran is many things, but she's never been a victim."

"Until now," Julia said after a sip of tea. "She's probably being put through the wringer at the station as we speak."

"Your gran can handle herself," he said with a smirk. "Imagine the chaos she's causing down there."

For the first time since the play, Julia laughed so naturally, it caught her by surprise. She almost felt guilty for laughing at such a time, but her father was right. She could see as clear as day how stressed the interviewing officers would be after spending an hour in her presence. She imagined each of them had been given a scorching dressing down in their first minute together.

"Do you think she did it?" Julia asked, her hands hugging her tea. "I mean, I know she *did it*, but do you think she did it knowingly?"

"My mother?" he said with a laugh. "Kill someone with a gun? Not in a million years."

Julia smiled at her father, glad she had someone on her side. At that moment, footsteps plodded across the marble tiles, and Katie walked into the kitchen, her platinum hair matted and her pink silk pyjamas stained.

"Coffee," she groaned. "Oh, hello, Julia. Sorry to hear about your gran."

Julia smiled her thanks as she finished the last of her tea. Not wanting to overstay her welcome with the new parents, she slid off the stool and joined Katie in staring down at Vinnie.

"I still can't believe he's mine," Katie beamed as she wrapped her hands around her body. "He's so perfect."

"Good genes," Brian said with a wink as he finished the last of the tea. "Go back to bed. I'll bring you up some coffee and lunch."

Katie let out a sigh of relief, kissed Brian on the lips, brushed Vinnie's hair, and patted Julia on the shoulder as she passed. She reached the archway before turning back and pointing at Julia.

"Do you want to have Christmas dinner here?" Katie asked. "Considering what's happening, I don't want you all without a place to go."

"Thank you, but no thank you," Julia said definitely. "We're going to have it at my gran's, just like every year. I'm going to get her out if it's the last thing I do."

Katie smiled sympathetically before shuffling up the cascading marble staircase. Julia grabbed her pink pea coat from the hat stand near the door as well as stuffing her feet back into her shoes.

"Don't get yourself into trouble," her father said as he hugged her goodbye. "Although I'm starting to think that trouble finds you wherever you go, Julia South."

"Me too, Dad," she said as she clung to his shirt. "Me too."

CHAPTER 6

Something sharp dug into Julia's neck, jolting her from her sleep. Her eyes sprang open to stare into Mowgli's as he rhythmically kneaded her over the covers, purring like a machine. Julia tickled the top of his head, prompting Mowgli to edge even closer. He rubbed his wet nose against her chin, his long white whiskers tickling her cheeks.

"Someone is happy to see you," Barker's voice

drifted from the doorway. "I knew I should have closed the door. He just couldn't resist."

"What time is it?" Julia asked as she sat up slightly, causing Mowgli to scurry away. "I feel like I've slept for days."

"Just gone eleven."

"Eleven?" Julia cried, bolting upright, catching her reflection in the mirror on top of her dressing table. "Why didn't you wake me up? It's my only day to –"

"Jessie turned off your alarm." Barker stepped into the room, already in his work suit. "She wanted you to sleep in for one Sunday in your life. She's been out shopping for ingredients for the café all morning, and last time I called her, she hadn't spent all your money on junk."

Barker sat on the edge of the bed and grabbed Julia's hand, a soft smile on his lips. Julia smiled back, almost forgetting why they had barely talked since butting heads at the village hall. When the sleep cleared, she remembered. She pulled her hand away, her eyes darting down.

"Is there any news?" she asked, her mind instantly turning to Dot. "How is she?"

"I hear she's in good spirits," Barker said. "She's officially been charged with murder but denied bail because of the seriousness of the crime. We're still gathering evidence to put a case together for when she goes to The Crown Court, but that can take months."

"*Months?*"

"The law is slow," Barker said with an apologetic shrug. "Unless we can prove without a doubt that she had no idea she was shooting a real gun, she's unlikely to be let out until her trial."

"So, you need a confession from the person who swapped the prop with a real gun?" Julia asked, the cogs in her mind whirring. "And then they'll let her out?"

"Julia…"

"What?" she cried. "My gran *needs* me."

Barker exhaled heavily as he stared down at the pattern on the duvet cover, his eyes dancing over the intricate design.

"It's not that simple," Barker said. "She *still* killed someone, but the charge can be dropped from murder to accidental or involuntary manslaughter. If that's the case, it's *very* possible she'll be let out on bail because she had no intention of killing anyone and will no longer be seen as dangerous, but it's still likely to go to trial and be decided by a jury."

"And then what?"

"Best case scenario, a fine."

"And worst case?"

Barker exhaled again, his eyes closing.

"Worst case, Barker?"

"Prison," he said solemnly. "I've seen people get weeks, I've seen people get months, and I've seen people get –"

"Years," Julia said with a gulp. "But she was just an eighty-three-year-old woman acting in a play."

"And that will work in her favour!" Barker said, grabbing Julia's hand again. "I wanted to tell you all of this on the night it happened, but I knew you wouldn't be able to look past the arrest. You know I couldn't do anything in that situation."

"I know," Julia said, suddenly feeling guilty for placing even a fraction of the blame for what happened on Barker. "But there's something *I* can do now. I can fix this, even if it's just to get her out for Christmas."

Barker nodded his understanding, and for a moment he looked like he was going to attempt to talk Julia out of getting involved, but he knew her better than that. She crawled across the bed and cuddled him, something she did not know she needed so badly until her face touched the side of his neck. They stayed like that until the house phone rang in the kitchen.

"No one rings the house phone," Barker said, pulling away from Julia.

"No one except my gran," Julia said as she launched off the bed, skidding out of her bedroom door like Mowgli running away from Jessie. She grabbed the phone from the wall in the kitchen and crammed it against her ear. "*Gran?* Gran, is that you?"

"Julia?" Dot's voice cried down the phone. "You're home! I didn't know whether I should ring here or the café and I didn't want to waste my phone call."

"Where are you?"

"In prison, dear!" Dot cried. "They've moved me. I'm '*banged up*', as they call it. It's rather different than what you expect. The food is better than anything I can cook, and my bed is rather comfy. The clothes are a little out of my comfort zone though. I'm currently wearing something one of the other girls called '*jogging bottoms*'. They're quite baggy, and I'm not sure I like them. You get used to the wind on your shins after so many years of wearing a skirt."

"Oh, Gran!" Julia cried as she fell backwards against the fridge, her eyes closed and a grin on her face. "I've missed you so much."

"That's so sweet of you," Dot replied with a laugh so pure, Julia could almost imagine her pushing up her curls at the back. "My lawyer has told me the police are doing everything they can to build my case, and I suspect you're giving them hell along the way."

"I'm going to get you out, Gran," Julia said, feeling like there was an invisible timer ticking down in the distance. "I promise. I'll figure this out."

"You can tell me all about that tomorrow," Dot said. "That's why I've called. They've let me have a visitor, and there's no one's hands I'd rather put my life in than yours. Can you come tomorrow?"

"Yes," Julia said quickly. "Yes, I'll be there."

After scribbling down an address and a contact phone number, Julia reluctantly said goodbye to her gran before replacing the phone on the wall. For a moment, she stared at the handset, the mixture of emotions dizzying. When she turned around, she was not surprised to see Barker waiting eagerly, having only heard one side of the conversation.

"She sounds fine," Julia said, the relief loud in her voice. "I can visit her tomorrow."

"That's wonderful news," Barker said, clapping his hands together. "See! Dot is a tough cookie.

She'll be ruling that prison by the end of the week. Let's go out for some lunch. I don't need to be at the station for another hour and a half."

Julia thought about her gran and how urgently she needed to start gathering information about where the cast and crew of the Peridale Amateur Dramatics Society all lived so she could start asking questions, but as she looked at Barker, she knew how desperately they needed some quality time together.

"I'll get dressed," Julia said before kissing him on the cheek. "I'll let you choose the place."

***

AFTER FINISHING A LARGE SLICE OF Christmas pie, which Julia deduced contained sausage meat, lemon, apricots, chestnuts, and thyme, she took a sip of her white wine, feeling all the better for getting out of the house and eating something substantial.

"Thank you for this," Julia said, grabbing Barker's hand across the table as she looked around The Plough, which was packed out with its usual Sunday afternoon punters. "I can't remember the last time we just came out for lunch."

"We both work so much," he said with a

regretful smile. "There's actually something I wanted to talk to you about regarding that."

Barker reached into the inside pocket of his jacket and began to pull out a letter, but he immediately slid it back when Evelyn, the eccentric owner of the B&B next door, drifted across the pub right towards them, her white kaftan floating ethereally behind her.

"*Julia*!" she cried, immediately clutching the green crystal chained around her neck. "How is your gran doing? I've been having terrible visions. I watched a documentary about a women's prison last week, and I can't help but think of all the terrible things that she's probably going through. I saw a woman get head-butted over a packet of chewing gum. Can you believe it? I've been asking the universe to protect her. I've been trying to send her positive energy and good vibrations, but I'm afraid it doesn't work so well if I don't have a specific location and postcode."

"She's doing great, Evelyn," Julia said, ignoring Barker's roll of his eyes, something most people did whenever Evelyn spoke. "I'm visiting her tomorrow. She sounded positive over the phone."

"Oh, that is lovely to hear," Evelyn said, reaching into her kaftan to pull out a satchel. "Give her this. It's a moonstone. If she holds onto it at night, it will protect her."

Evelyn dropped a small pearlescent stone the size and shape of a marble in Julia's hand. She rolled it around in her hand, the colour shifting like oil in water.

"It's beautiful," Julia said as she clasped her hand around the stone. "I'll pass it on."

"You'll never get that into a prison," Barker whispered over his pint. "It looks like drugs."

Julia shot Barker a look that silenced him immediately before she turned to Evelyn, who either did not hear or chose not to.

"I've got one for each of the cast and crew," Evelyn said as she gave the same bag a shake. "I've studied each of their auras and decided what stone will save them most."

"You have their addresses?" Julia asked, sitting up suddenly. "I was hoping to speak to some of them."

"I was just going to pop into the rehearsal," Evelyn said as she pushed the small bag into a hidden pocket within her reams of fabric. "I hope they won't mind me barging in, but I do come bearing gifts, although isn't there a parable telling you to beware of the Greek who comes bearing gifts?

I'm a quarter Greek on my mother's side, so maybe I should stay away after –"

"*Rehearsal?*" Julia said, jumping in. "What rehearsal?"

"Oh, well I suppose they're rehearsing at the village hall right now," Evelyn said as she tapped on the middle of her forehead. "My third eye isn't that specific, but I assumed they were after I heard tomorrow's performance was going ahead."

"How?" Barker jumped in, looking as confused as Julia felt. "Their leading man is dead, and their leading lady is behind bars."

"You know what, I completely forgot to ask," Evelyn said with a wave of her hand as she giggled. "I'd better go. My grandson, Mark, is waiting for me at the B&B. We're renovating a room for him, so he has somewhere to stay that's his own when his father goes on those tours with that tribute band he's part of. Give my love to Dot."

Evelyn floated away like a puff of smoke, vanishing as quickly as she had appeared.

"Julia –"

"Thanks for lunch," she said, screwing up the napkin from her knee and dropping it on the empty plate. "I'll see you after you've finished work."

Leaving Barker to finish his pint in The Plough,

Julia hurried across the village, choosing to walk around the village green, which had turned to icy sludge since the snow had started falling and begun to melt. When she reached the church grounds, she heard the unmistakable sound of a gun firing. She sprinted towards the door, bursting through with a thud.

"*Cut*!" Ross cried as all eyes turned to Julia as she stood at the back of the hall, staring at her gran's replacement holding the prop. "Carlton, is it possible to start locking those doors?"

The man playing Jimmy sat up and pulled his wig off to scratch his thick hair underneath. He only looked to be in his twenties, and Julia was sure she recognised him as one of the crew who had run around backstage on opening night. To her surprise, Darcy pulled off her brown wig, revealing Catherine's blonde hair, and Mandy's blonde wig vanished to show Poppy's red hair.

"Can we smoke in here?" Catherine cried out as she pulled a packet of cigarettes from her pocket and placed one between her lips. When no one responded, she shrugged and lit the cigarette before sitting at the table to flick through a script. Poppy meekly backed away, heading to the lighting booth, where Jayesh was waiting for her.

"What do you want?" Ross demanded as he marched towards Julia in a bright pink silk shirt, unbuttoned down the middle to reveal a well worked out and slightly hairy chest. "Your family has caused enough trouble. If you're here about the gingerbread men, I looked over the agreement, and you said you'd do them as a gesture of goodwill, so it's too late to start demanding money."

"I'm not here about money," Julia said, stiffening her spine. "I'm going to be honest with you. I don't believe my gran fired that gun intentionally, and I believe someone in your club replaced the gun to conveniently frame her. Now, you can either co-operate and let me ask some questions, or you can tell me to leave, in which case, I will remind you that this is a *community* village hall and I have every right to be here, and I will exercise that right, and I won't do it peacefully."

Ross crossed his arms over his bulky chest as he grinned at Julia with a raised eyebrow.

"I like you," he said, circling a finger around Julia's face. "Very dramatic. You're your grandmother's granddaughter alright. Have you ever thought about acting? Your delivery is *quite* something. Come with me. I will talk to you."

Ross turned on his heels, the soles of his shoes

squeaking on the polished floor. Carlton shot daggers across the room from the doorway of his cleaning storeroom, but he soon darted out when Catherine's cigarette triggered the smoke alarm. Leaving Carlton to fan the smoke with an old towel, they slipped backstage and into one of the side rooms, which seemed to be a makeshift office for Ross.

He waited for Julia to walk in, closed the door behind him, and planted himself in a chair in front of a paper-covered desk. He attempted to straighten up some of the piles, but he gave up with a wave of his hand.

"Some people call it messy, but I call it bursting with ideas," Ross said as he reached into a mini fridge under the desk. "Sparkling water?"

"No, thank you," Julia said, standing awkwardly by the door, her hands clasped together in front of her. "I really just want to talk about your uncle."

"What do you want to know?" Ross asked as he poured sparkling water from a green bottle into a small glass. "Didn't really know the man all that well, despite him being my only surviving blood relative. I guess it's just me now. My parents died when I was young, and I was raised by my grandfather. Marvellous man. Nothing like my uncle. I think my grandfather resented Marcus going to prison until the day he died. Grandfather was an army man. Disciplined and respectful. He always said his greatest regret in life was not knowing where he went wrong raising Marcus."

Julia resisted reaching into her bag to pull out her notepad, instead repeating the key facts over and over in her mind, hoping they stuck; she was just grateful Ross was opening up at all.

"So, you know about what he did to my gran?"

"I didn't know it was *her*," he said after a sip of his water. "They hid it well. I guess that's what happens when you mature. It happened so long ago. I found your grandmother at a Christmas market. She was animated and yelling the whole tent to the ground. I saw her, and I said, '*I want her to star in my Christmas show*'. It was a stroke of luck, really. That was only two weeks after I took the position of director. Bertha Bloom, bless her, is as batty as a box of frogs and nice enough, but she didn't know a thing about directing a play. I bumped into Marcus a couple of months ago in a bar. It was a pure coincidence, but he told me about his fears of doing another awful Christmas play, and I had just left my job working for a theatre company in London. I needed something to occupy my mind, and I thought resurrecting a dead am-dram club would look great on my CV. Bertha didn't put up much of a fight, so we got to work at the beginning of November."

"Are you close to your aunt?"

"You mean Catherine?" he snorted. "That woman is *not* my aunt, and if I had my way, she never would have been in the play. When I turned up here to start work, he introduced her as his wife. They've only been married since the summer. They met on holiday, and I suspect he told her about his riches and her eyes glazed over. Marcus insisted I give her a part, so I did. She promoted herself to Darcy's character, but there wasn't much I could do. She knows the lines, even if her delivery is awful, but what am I supposed to do? The shooting has sold out the rest of the shows. Interest is so hot, I've started selling standing tickets too, just to cram as many people in as possible. Whether we're positively reviewed or not, it will end up being a sold-out run."

"Have you thought about who could have switched the guns?" Julia asked. "Or why?"

"Now you're starting to sound like the police," he said as he stood up, finishing off the last of his water. "They've questioned us all a handful of times already, but no one is talking. If someone here did it, they're better actors than I thought."

As though letting Julia know her time was up, Ross opened the door and waited patiently until she walked through it. Satisfied with what she had heard, she headed back to the front of the stage, leaving Ross in his office. She was pleased when she spotted Poppy sitting alone in the front row seats, the blonde wig in her lap as she mouthed along to her lines on her script.

"Poppy, isn't it?" Julia asked softly as she sat next to the redhead. "I'm not interrupting, am I?"

"I'm just going over my lines," she said, squinting at Julia, clearly not much older than Jessie. "Can I help you?"

"You can," Julia said with a nod, glancing down at the script, which was full of Ross' scribbles. "Why were you crying at the dress rehearsal, and then again during the opening night?"

"Oh," Poppy said, clearly shocked by Julia's bluntness. "I – I was just nervous."

"But you were only working backstage, weren't you?"

"I – I don't know," she said quickly, looking down at her script but clearly not reading it. "I don't remember."

Julia rested her hand on Poppy's, which

shuddered under her touch. Julia smiled at her, hoping the young girl would trust her enough to be honest.

"I saw you in Marcus' dressing room before the performance," Julia whispered, glancing around the village hall to make sure they were not being overheard. "You don't have to keep a dead man's secret."

Poppy stared at Julia as though she had just heard the most terrifying thing in her life. When Jayesh walked over, Poppy immediately jumped up, dropping the wig and the script on the floor.

"Everything okay?" Jayesh asked. "Hello, Julia."

"Everything is fine," Julia said with a smile at the post office owner's eldest son. "Say hello to your mother for me when you go home."

Jayesh nodded that he would as he looked from Julia to Poppy.

"It was nothing," Poppy whispered to Julia. "I was *just* nervous."

Jayesh stared down at Julia for a moment before leading Poppy off, his hand on the small of her back, giving Julia the impression they were an item. She turned her attention to Catherine, who was reading over her script at the kitchen table on the set, her fingers drumming on her packet of cigarettes.

"Let's reset and start from the beginning of Act Two!" Ross called out, clapping his hands together as he resumed his seat at the front of the stage. "Places, people! Places!"

Realising she was not going to get anything else out of these people as long as they were rehearsing, Julia gave in and headed for the front door. She did not need to turn around to know Carlton was following her with a mop.

CHAPTER 7

Julia woke early the next morning before sunrise, Evelyn's moonstone clutched in her palm. She quickly baked some cakes for the café, wolfed down some toast, dropped Jessie off in the village, and set off for her visit with Dot.

Julia had never visited a prison, nor had she ever expected to, so her expectations were widely based on what she had seen on television and in films. Her drive to Eastwood Park Women's Prison took her to Wotton-under-Edge, a quaint picturesque town only half an hour away from Peridale. As she drove through the narrow streets lined with shops and cafés, she checked the sat-nav more than once to make sure it was taking her the right way.

"*Take the next right down Church Lane*," the robotic voice announced. "*Your destination is on the right.*"

Julia passed a beautiful church, not unlike St. Peter's Church in the heart of Peridale. She followed the winding tree-lined road as the navigator had directed, her eyes peeled for a sudden looming concrete structure. What she got was something entirely different. As Julia pulled into the small visitor's car park across the road, she looked at the collection of buildings through her rear-view mirror, which without the high green fence, could have been a community centre or a school. If Julia had driven past on a quiet Sunday, she would not have thought she was passing a prison.

Julia jumped out of her car at the same time as another woman across the car park did. They shared a brief smile, a smile Julia quickly came to realise was one only two women about to visit relatives in a prison could share. Julia's nerves set in all of a sudden, giving her the urge to jump back into her car so she could drive back to Peridale and pretend none of this was happening.

"First time?" the woman called from across the car park as Julia found that she was pinning herself against the back of her aqua blue Ford Anglia. "I haven't seen you here before."

"Oh," Julia mumbled with a nod. "I'm visiting my gran."

"My sister," the woman announced. "Killed her husband by whacking him around the head with an iron. He'd been abusing her for twenty years, but that's the justice system for you. Come with me. I'll show you the ropes."

Julia joined the woman, who she quickly learned was called Brenda, grateful she did not have to face this alone. They walked up to the visitor entrance, where they flashed their IDs and visitor cards, the latter of which Julia did not have. The guard in the small box looked at her suspiciously before finding her name on a separate list on the computer system. When he was satisfied Julia was who she said she was, he buzzed them into a slender metal outdoor corridor, which he instructed them to follow to the door at the end.

Julia tried to soak in every inch of the prison as

Brenda told her how she had been visiting her sister every week for six years. Side by side with a chattering Brenda, all Julia could think of as they walked towards the door was how much smaller and less threatening the place looked than she had imagined.

"It doesn't look like a prison," Julia whispered to Brenda when they reached the door. "Are they all like this?"

"Your gran got lucky," she whispered back as she opened the door. "This is one of the good ones."

They walked into a small pale-pink reception area, which looked like it could have been a doctor's waiting room, complete with similar posters warning about anti-social behaviour towards staff, and, more obviously prison-orientated ones, warning about the dangers of attempting to smuggle in contraband.

After signing in at the desk, they were instructed to sit and wait. Julia and Brenda chatted about Christmas and the weather, as though visiting prison was just a normal part of their day. It put Julia at ease. She wondered how different the experience would have been if she had arrived five minutes earlier or later and had to do it alone.

After fifteen minutes, both of their names were called. They were directed to an airport style scanner, where they were instructed to empty all pockets, remove any loose items of clothing and shoes, and asked to check the list of items they were not allowed to take into the prison. Julia's phone, handbag, and car keys were put in a small zip-lock bag, and her scarf and coat were taken into a storeroom to be held. After being scanned, and patted down by the woman guard who did not look like she had smiled a single day in her life, she was given a tray with her shoes and the moonstone after they had been checked. Before she grabbed the moonstone, the guard picked it up and inspected it after spotting it rattling around the tray.

"What's this?" the guard asked, staring suspiciously down at the pearlescent ball. "Are you trying to sneak something through?"

"It's a moonstone," she explained.

"What does it do?" the guard asked as she rolled it around between her fingers up to the light. "What's in it?"

"It doesn't do anything," Julia said. "Not really. It's for good luck. A friend asked me to pass it onto my gran. It's just a stone."

"Sorry," the guard said as she dropped it into a plastic zip-lock bag. "You can have it back before you leave."

Julia did not argue, especially when she caught Brenda giving her a little head shake. She knew her gran did not believe in Evelyn's mystic ways, but Julia was sure she had slept a little easier the night before holding the stone in her hand.

After putting on her shoes, Julia re-joined Brenda before walking through another series of doors, followed by the visitors who had arrived after them. They waited in a small holding room, which looked out onto the visiting room, which was also painted pale pink. Small tables with chairs were dotted around the room, looking more like an informal café than somewhere to sit with criminals. There were even vending machines lining one of the walls.

"Here," Brenda said, placing a small yellow token in Julia's hand. "It's for the vending machine. They don't give you these until they learn your face, but I don't always use them, so I've got some spare ones."

Julia accepted it with a grateful smile, sure a cup of tea was just what she needed. Before she could ask any more questions, a loud buzzer echoed around the room, and the door in front of them clicked.

"Here we go," Brenda said. "Good luck, and savour it. We don't get nearly long enough."

Before either Brenda or Julia could move, a much younger woman rushed forward and burst through the crowd. On the other side of the room, another door opened, and a group of women of diverse ages in similar grey jumpers and jogging bottoms walked in. When the young girl spotted the woman she was looking for, they hugged for as long as they could before a voice announced over the speaker that hugs should last five seconds and no longer.

Julia walked in cautiously, spotting her gran amongst the faces. Julia could not help but run up to her, just like the young woman before her. She grabbed her gran in the tightest hug she had ever given her, forgetting all about the five-second rule. She only pulled away when one of the wardens tapped her on the shoulder with a baton.

"Oh, Julia," Dot said as they sat at one of the tables. "I'd almost forgotten your face. How long has it been?"

"Four days, Gran."

"Are you *sure*?" Dot replied, frowning across the table, her eyes distant. "I've lost all track of time. I can barely remember what Peridale looks like."

Julia chuckled, glad her gran had not lost her sense of drama and overreaction. They cupped hands across the table, until another warden reminded them not to touch each other. Julia's mind was full of questions, but she could feel an invisible clock ticking away as she stared at her gran's face, which looked so different in the grey jumper. Without her stiff collar and brooch, she looked like a different woman entirely.

"How is it in here?" Julia asked, unsure if she even wanted to know the answer. "It's a lot nicer than I expected."

"Honestly?" Dot replied, locking eyes with Julia. "It's bloody marvellous!"

"It is?"

"Oh, yes," Dot said as she pushed up her curls at the back. "Everyone is so lovely. Apparently, they go easier on us older girls. I have three hot meals a day, a comfortable bed, and there's even a TV room. I feel like I'm going to get caught up on all my shows in here. Oh, and there's a library, and classes. I did yoga this morning."

"Yoga?

"Oh, it's all the rage in here," Dot said with a nod. "Some of these girls can get their legs into some peculiar positions! I feel ten years younger."

"You don't sound like you're in any rush to get out," Julia said, her voice faltering. "I miss you."

"And I miss you too, dear," Dot said, reaching across and running her finger across Julia's cheek, quickly retreating before they were told off again. "I could be in here for a while, so I might as well make the most of it. My perm curls will start dropping in a month, so I'll see how I feel then. But, I've got to face the facts. I *did* shoot a man."

"But not on purpose," Julia said, unsure if she was making a statement or asking a question. "Why didn't you tell me about your connection with Marcus?"

"Because I didn't hold a grudge," Dot said with a wave of her hand as though it was nothing. "I suppose you've been filled in on everything that happened. I can't tell you how many times I visualised killing him in the early days. I was so embarrassed that I'd allowed myself to be taken for a fool. When he came out of prison, I made a point of letting go. Hating someone is like eating a poisonous apple and expecting *them* to die. I didn't want to be that person, so I simply let it go."

Dot trickled her fingers up to the ceiling as though she was talking about forgiving someone for taking the last slice of cake at her birthday party.

"We don't have long," Julia said, Brenda's words ringing out in her ears. "I need to know about the gun."

"Oh, it did feel so much heavier!" Dot announced loudly. "I thought it was my nerves, but I should have looked a little closer. The second I pulled the trigger, I knew what I'd done. Marcus is a brilliant actor, but he's not *that* good."

"Did you know you'd be acting across from him?"

"Not until after my audition," Dot said, her finger tapping on her chin as she thought back. "I told Ross I wasn't so sure about working with Marcus. It's one thing to forgive, but you don't ever forget. Ross was right about it adding to the chemistry though. Our history gave us both something to draw from. We tapped into that resentment and brought it to life on the stage. It's such a shame the village will never get to see the rest of the play."

"I think they will," Julia whispered after a gulp. "They're continuing with a new cast."

"*What?*" Dot cried, sitting up suddenly in her chair. "But they can't! I *am* Darcy! Who've they replaced me with?"

"Catherine," Julia said quickly. "And Poppy is playing Catherine's role."

"That *slime!*" Dot cried, screwing up her fist and

slamming it down on the small table, catching the attention of the patrolling warden. "How *dare* she! I wouldn't be surprised if she set the whole thing up to take my spot."

"Do you think she'd do that?" Julia asked. "I need to know as much as possible about everyone if I'm going to solve this."

Dot smiled her appreciation across the table, even if it was laced with sadness. Julia did not need to ask where the sadness came from to understand; as Dot had said, she had killed someone.

"Catherine is an interfering busybody," Dot said. "She was always trying to give me notes on how to improve my performance. I couldn't stand the scenes we were in together. I didn't have to try hard to get across my hatred for Mandy Smith trying to steal my husband. In reality, what would a woman like her, still young enough, pretty and blonde, see in a man like Marcus Miller, with his bald head and gut? Money, that's what! Classic gold digger. You know they met on holiday? I bet she was waiting by the bar for the first sad, lonely old man to catch her eyes. I bet she took one look at his designer watch and sniffed out his riches."

"Marcus was rich?"

"Oh, yes!" Dot said with a definite nod. "He

gained his fortune legitimately though, so I can't knock him for that. When you spend that long rehearsing with someone, you get to know them even if you don't particularly like them. He was always taking business phone calls. He said he owned a whole bunch of houses in London, and you know what house prices are like down there. I think he rented them out, so he was raking in the cash, and I'd bet his property assets were in the millions. He did the Christmas plays because he loved acting so much. Our mutual love of being on the stage was the one thing we could see eye to eye on."

"So, Catherine would have a lot to gain from Marcus' death, wouldn't she?" Julia said, wishing she had been allowed to bring her notepad and pen in. "Did he have any connections to the rest of the cast?"

"Not that I can think of," Dot said, her finger tapping rhythmically on her chin as the cogs worked in her mind. "He wasn't particularly popular. He was a bossy perfectionist. He's been in the club for years, so he knows how things are done. I think that's why he and Ross worked so well. They both had clear visions of the play and how it should come across. I can't imagine the rest of the shows are going to be very good with Catherine Miller playing Darcy

Monroe! What a *mess*!"

"What do you know about Poppy?" Julia asked, suddenly remembering what she had seen before the first performance. "Does she have a connection to Marcus?"

"Poppy is studying drama at college, although I think she was more interested in the backstage stuff. She's far too meek to be up on that stage. I dread to think what the pressure of being Mandy Smith is doing to her. She's frail. Nothing like I was at that age. She needs to get a backbone. Cries an awful lot."

"I saw something the night of the performance," Julia whispered, leaning across the table. "I saw Poppy in Marcus' dressing room. He looked like he was trying to kiss her. She ran off crying, just like she did in the dress rehearsal the day before."

"Trying to *kiss* her?" Dot cried. "That dirty old man! She's so young. She and that post office lady's son are courting, or so it seems. Poor girl."

"I've tried talking to her, but she insists it was just first night nerves," Julia said. "I think she's scared to admit it. Do you think he could have been trying to seduce her?"

Dot thought for a moment, her tapping finger speeding up. She clicked her fingers together suddenly, making Julia jump.

"Now that I think of it, the only time I saw her not a quivering wreck was the day Marcus had a cold and couldn't come to rehearsals," Dot said as she slowly nodded. "He would always shout at her every time she missed her cues. I think she was just there because she loved the theatre, like when I was her age, but I didn't even think there could be something else going on. I feel so awful."

"Don't," Julia said. "Men like that get away with these things because they pick on the girls they know will be too terrified to speak out. If I can just get it out of her –"

"Then she's got a motive to kill him," Dot said, her eyes widening. "She could have theoretically switched the guns."

"Anyone could have," Julia said. "But yes, it would give her a motive."

Dot sank into her chair, not seeming thrilled by the idea that a young woman would take her place if the scenario was true. Before either of them could say any more, a buzzer jolted through the room and a voice announced that visitors should say their goodbyes and make their way back to the holding room.

"Don't worry about me," Dot whispered as she

hugged Julia. "I can handle myself in here."

"I'm going to find out the truth, Gran," Julia assured her. "No matter what it is. You can't spend the rest of your life in here for someone else's crime."

"Pass on my love to everyone," Dot said, squeezing Julia one last time before she pulled away. "Be safe, Julia."

Dot drifted away, following the group of identically dressed women back into the prison. She looked back before she vanished to give Julia a small smile.

"How did it go?" Brenda asked when they were back in the reception area waiting for their items to be handed back. "Not scared you away, has it?"

"I don't think I'll be coming back here," Julia said certainly. "I'm going to get her out."

Brenda arched a brow at Julia, her smile letting Julia know she thought she was crazy. When Brenda's items were handed back, she hurried out of the prison without saying another word to Julia. With the moonstone in her hand, Julia sat in one of the chairs as she refilled her coat pockets with her things.

She pulled her phone out of the plastic bag, surprised to see seven missed calls from Jessie, along with a text message: '*Kim is here!!!! @ the café!!! Not gud. Hurry up xx'*

CHAPTER 8

As Julia drove back to Peridale, snow slowly drifted from the pale sky, dusting everything in another blanket of white like a freshly baked Victoria sponge cake sprinkled with a layer of icing sugar. After pulling into the parking space between her café and the post office, Julia hurried into the warmth where Kim was seated at the table nearest the counter, looking over the contents of a file.

Julia unravelled her scarf as she walked across the warm room, the scent of cinnamon and hot cocoa in the air. It seemed that the rest of Peridale's inhabitants were staying in the warmth of their homes because the only customer aside from Kim was Evelyn, who appeared to be giving herself a tarot reading.

"Julia!" Kim exclaimed as she looked up, snapping the file shut. "There you are!"

Kim was wearing a bright red and green Christmas jumper with a rigid denim skirt and fluffy snow boots. The butterfly clips in her hair had been replaced with small slides depicting Rudolph's face. Her lips were covered in badly applied glittery pink lipstick, but she still had the frosted blue eye shadow. Her smile looked a lot more strained than at their last meeting.

"I'm so sorry, Kim," Julia started as she shrugged off her pink coat. "I had some errands to run. I hope you haven't been waiting too long. I didn't realise we had a meeting today. Can I get you anything?"

"She's already had three mince pies," Jessie announced. "And two hot chocolates."

"I was just passing," Kim said, her fingers

drumming on the file. "Had some business over on the Fern Moore estate. I saw a newspaper headline there that caught my attention."

Kim reached into her purple handbag and pulled out the edition of *The Peridale Post* announcing Dot's '*revenge*'. Julia gulped as she stared down at the picture of Dot's hand blocking the camera. She hurried around the counter, hung up her coat and scarf, swapping them for her Christmas themed Mrs Claus apron.

"Is it a problem?" Julia asked casually as she checked over the stock levels in the display fridge.

"Yes, it's a problem!" Kim cried shrilly, her eyes dancing to the pile of fresh mince pies in the fridge before they snapped on Julia. "Your grandmother has been charged with murder! I feel like I should know things like this."

"She's not been convicted," Jessie cried as she scowled at Kim. "This is what you *always* do! Your fingers are firmly on that rug, and you're about to pull it right from under me."

Kim's eyes snapped to Jessie, her glittery lips pouting like a little girl who had just been told off by her mother. Kim stiffened her spine as she stood up, her rigid skirt jutting out at her calves in an unfashionable way.

"I was just passing to let you both know that I will be looking into this further and it might slow down, or even hinder your adoption application."

"But that's not fair!" Jessie cried, beating her hands down on the counter. "You're such a dumb –"

"It's all just a big misunderstanding," Julia jumped in before Jessie got them into further trouble. "Someone switched the gun to frame my gran for the murder."

"Has this been proven?" Kim asked, glancing again at the newspaper article. "It sounds like she planned the whole thing quite meticulously, if you ask me."

"We *didn't* ask you," Jessie snapped with a roll of her eyes. "We're going to prove she was stitched up. Dot didn't murder him."

"Well, that remains to be seen," Kim said as she wandered over to the display cabinet, her eyes firmly on the mince pies. "Crimes like this are serious, especially when they're committed by close family members. It casts everything in a very different light and makes me want to reconsider the suitability of this adoption."

"You can't force me to leave," Jessie cried. "I'm over sixteen. I'm a young adult. I should be out of care by now anyway."

"That is true," Kim said to the mince pies. "I'll take two of these to go."

Julia reluctantly bagged up two mince pies, making sure to charge Kim full price for both of them.

"When my gran is found to be innocent, will it still matter?" Julia asked as she passed Kim her change.

"*If* that happens, we might be able to overlook it. But time is running out for this adoption to be finalised in time for Jessie's eighteenth birthday, so unless you get a signed and sealed confession from this so-called person who framed your gran, you might miss the deadline altogether."

With that, Kim turned on her heels and plodded out of the café, dropping her mince pies on the ground the second she was out of the door. One of them rolled out of the brown paper bag, but she quickly scooped it up, blew off the snow, and bit into it.

"I *told* you something would happen," Jessie said, her hands tensing into fists on the counter. "I *hate* her."

"We'll fix this," Julia said as she rested a hand on Jessie's shoulder. "Dot *will* be out for Christmas. I'll make sure of it."

Jessie sighed before doubling back and heading into the kitchen. Julia decided to let her have a moment, so she started wiping down the tables.

"I couldn't help but overhear," Evelyn whispered as she adjusted her berry red turban. "You know you don't need a piece of paper for Jessie to be your daughter. I see your auras very clearly, and it is definitely one of mother and daughter. You both remind me so much of Astrid and me, God rest her soul."

"Thank you, Evelyn," Julia replied as she picked up Evelyn's empty cup. "Salted caramel latte? Let me get you a refill on the house."

While Julia got to work making Evelyn's drink, the bell above the door rang out, and Johnny Watson walked in, a sheepish smile on his face. His dark curls peeked out in tufts from under a red Santa Claus hat, and he was holding what looked like a charity collection pot.

"Can you believe it's only a week to go?" Johnny asked as he approached the counter, his eyes trained on the chalkboard menu on the wall behind Julia. "It comes around quicker every year."

"Can I make you a drink?" Julia offered as she poured the milk into Evelyn's latte. "The gingerbread hot chocolate has been especially popular this year."

"I can't stop," he said, shaking the small charity pot. "My editor has sent me out collecting for *The Peridale Post* charity drive. We're raising money for the children's hospital, but our readers are getting less and less generous every year, so we keep falling short of our targets. I was just passing, and I wanted to talk to you about the case."

Julia took Evelyn her latte as she was digging in a tiny purse. Evelyn pulled out a ten-pound note and slotted it into Johnny's charity pot.

"Anything for kiddies," she said with a soft smile. "I'll be asking the universe to send healthy energy their way tonight."

"Thank you," Johnny said as he sat in the seat nearest the counter pulling the strap of his bag over his head. "I've been walking around the village all morning going door to door, and you've just doubled the total."

"Consider it tripled," Julia said as she pulled a ten-pound note from the petty cash tin under the counter. "What did you want to talk to me about?"

Julia popped a peppermint and liquorice tea bag into a cup, filled it with hot water, and sat across from Johnny. He pulled off his Santa hat before pulling a stack of photocopied newspaper articles from his bag. He slapped them on the table, his handwritten notes filling the margins.

"I still feel awful about having to write that piece about your gran," Johnny said as he fiddled with his glasses, his pale cheeks turning red. "I feel like people have clung to that story and used it as a way to blame her without looking at other potential motives."

"The police will have made the connection without you," Julia reminded him as she blew on the hot tea. "You have papers to sell."

Johnny pulled a paperclip from the corner of the papers before flicking through them. When he landed on the one he wanted, he slid it across the counter to Julia; it was an obituary page, and one entry had been circled in red pen.

"I've been looking into the other members of the group," he said, an excited smile shaking his lips. "Nothing suspicious jumped out at first, but I'm a journalist, so it's my job to read between the lines."

"'*Martin Tucker, aged 85, died on Sunday, September 23rd, 2014*,'" Julia read aloud from the clipping. "'*Son of famous Politician, Jonathan Tucker, Martin served northern town Accrington as MP for The Labour Party between 1984 and 1992. He is survived by his wife, Catherine Tucker, 41, and his two sons, Simon Tucker and Harry Tucker, 52 and 59 respectively*'."

"I stumbled upon it by accident," Johnny said. "I was cross-referencing Catherine Miller's date of birth with other Catherines, and I found this one. She's been married more times than I've had hot dinners. Here's another one."

Johnny pulled out a second obituary, this time about sixty-nine-year-old French restaurant millionaire tycoon Louis Bernard, leaving behind his thirty-nine-year-old wife, Catherine Bernard. He pulled out a third, this time Jack Harris, seventy-one, leaving behind his thirty-four-year-old wife, Catherine Harris.

"This is all the same Catherine as Marcus' wife?" Julia asked as she looked over the obituaries. "Are you sure?"

"Born Catherine Marsh in 1972," Johnny stated as he read from another sheet of paper. "Father was a miner, mother was a housewife. She was the middle child of seven and the only girl. Married her first husband, David Power, in 1990 when she was eighteen, and he was twenty-nine. They were married for twelve years but divorced in 2002, with David claiming she had been '*unfaithful with multiple partners*'. Over the course of their marriage,

David amassed a fortune in the taxi business, but she walked away with nothing thanks to some good lawyers. David is the only one of her husband's *not* to have died. She married Jack in 2003, and he died in 2006, she married Louis in 2009, and he died in 2011, she married Martin in 2013, and he died in 2014, and finally, she married Marcus in July 2017, and he died last week. Five husbands in five different parts of the country, all of them wealthy in their own way, and four of them now dead."

Johnny passed over his handwritten notes summarising everything she had just heard. She read over them quickly, soaking in every last detail.

"This is incredible," Julia whispered, unable to believe what she was reading. "And she's got away with this every time?"

"Well, here's the thing," Johnny said, pulling out a second piece of paper. "I obviously noticed the pattern too, so I went digging even further. Jack died of surgery complications getting his fourth facelift, thanks to a pre-existing lung condition, Louis was a lifelong diabetic who ignored his condition and died from heart disease, Martin had cancer when he met Catherine, and the whole village saw what happened to Marcus."

"So, you're saying it's a coincidence all her

husbands died, and she inherited their fortunes?"

"I'm saying, she *clearly* had a type," Johnny pulled out a wad of wedding pictures and spread them on the table, each depicting a not-so-healthy looking man with a woman with a different hair colour in each picture. "What if she sought out men who were ill, or even dying, made them fall in love with her, took their money, and ran off into the sunset with a bottle of hair dye to do it all again somewhere else."

"Is that legal?"

"It's not *il*legal," Johnny said with a shrug as he tapped his finger on one of the pictures showing one of the unlucky husbands in a wheelchair with oxygen tubes up his nose. "This is Martin. They met in a private cancer hospital, where she was his *nurse*. Checked it out, and there's an open investigation because she faked her qualifications."

"She's a con-woman."

"A very good one too," Johnny said, almost impressed. "She doesn't stay anywhere too long, never looks the same, and in between cons goes by dozens of different names. Even if these men searched for her online, they wouldn't find any of this. It's my job to find this stuff, and even I struggled."

"Do you think she switched the guns to kill Marcus and take his money?" Julia asked, her head spinning with all of the new information. "That doesn't really fit the pattern, does it?"

"It doesn't, but I found Marcus' lawyer and called pretending to be a distant relative," Johnny said with a pleased grin. "The will is being read tomorrow, per his wife's request."

Julia nodded as she looked over the papers on the table.

"Can I have a copy of these?" Julia asked, not wanting the information to leave her side. "This is all really helpful."

"This *is* your copy," Johnny said with a wink. "I made two of everything for this very reason. Investigating Catherine's past has taken me days, but I've not finished digging up information about the rest of the cast and crew."

"Keep up the brilliant work," Julia said as she gathered up the papers. "I had my suspicions about Catherine before, but this has kicked things up a notch."

"Do you think she did it?" Johnny asked, standing up and putting his messenger bag over his head. "I've been thinking about taking this stuff to the police before she flees the village."

"Don't," Julia said firmly. "We need a concrete confession if my gran stands a chance of having her charges reduced. It needs proving beyond any doubt."

"How are you going to get a confession?" Johnny asked as he sandwiched the hat back on his head.

"I haven't figured that part out yet," Julia said after a sip of the peppermint and liquorice tea. "I'm sure I'll think of something. Thank you for this, Johnny. Don't let anyone tell you you're not brilliant."

With blushing cheeks, Johnny headed back to the door with the charity pot in his hand, a pleased smile on his face. As he turned around, he bumped into Barker before scurrying off.

"Someone looked like they were in a good mood," Barker said, closing the door behind him as he watched Johnny hurry across the village green. "Did you finally agree to go on a proper date with him?"

"Very funny," Julia said as she straightened up the bundle of papers. "He was just collecting money for the newspaper, and he has found some very interesting information on Catherine Miller, or should I say, Catherine Marsh-Power-Harris-

Bernard-Tucker-Miller?"

Barker arched a brow at Julia out of the corner of his eye as he leaned into the display cabinet to look at what was on offer.

"What are you talking about?" Barker asked with a confused smile. "Where's the chocolate cake?"

Jessie appeared from the kitchen with a slice of Barker's favourite double chocolate fudge cake, of which Julia always made sure to have extra in the kitchen fridge. Barker picked it up with a wink before taking the seat across from Julia.

"Catherine has had five husbands," Julia said, pushing the file across to Barker. "All dead, apart from her first. I suppose you haven't looked that deeply into it yet, have you?"

"It's not my case," Barker mumbled through a mouthful of chocolate cake. "Chief decided I was too close to it to be unbiased, especially with – well, with *your* reputation. He thought I might be feeding you information."

"And yet here I am," Julia said, reaching across to wipe chocolate icing off Barker's chin. "Feeding you information from Johnny Watson, a measly journalist."

Barker took another bite of the chocolate cake as he flicked through the paperwork, squinting at the glossy wedding photographs.

"Can I keep this?" Barker mumbled through a mouthful of cake. "I could pass it on to the investigation team. Might help your gran's case."

"No." Julia pulled back the file in a flash. "I have a feeling it will be too easy to spin any information into making my gran look guiltier. If they want this, they can figure it out for themselves."

Barker smirked before taking another bite of the cake.

"I suppose you won't want to know the information I just heard in the bathroom then, would you?"

Julia tucked the file into her handbag behind the counter before slowly rising up to look at Barker. Evelyn, who was still shuffling through tarot cards and picking them out at random was clearly eavesdropping on the entire conversation, and had probably been doing the same throughout Johnny's.

"Shoot," Julia said as she leaned against the counter.

"Forensics pulled two sets of fingerprints off the gun," Barker said as he wiped chocolate from the corners of his mouth with the back of his hand. "One belonged to Dot, and another to an unknown person."

"How is that useful?" Julia asked.

"They don't belong to anyone on file," Barker said, pushing the plate away. "But it's only a matter of time before they fingerprint everyone who was at the village hall that night and get a match."

"But most of the village was there," Evelyn called out, immediately sinking into her chair. "I mean, or so I heard. A play about murder didn't really interest me."

Julia thought about the information for a second, but it didn't intrigue her as much as the file Johnny had given her. A fingerprint could belong to anyone, and it could take days if not weeks until they matched it.

"There was something I wanted to tell you, actually," Barker said as he reached into his pocket to pull something out. "I've been meaning to tell you all week, but –"

Before Barker could finish his sentence, the smoke alarm in the kitchen began blaring. Julia ran into the kitchen just in time to see Jessie pulling a blackened tray of gingerbread men from the oven with a sheepish smile.

"Forgot about them," she said as she dumped them in the sink before dousing them with water. "Oops."

After opening the back door and fanning at the smoke alarm with a towel, Julia walked back into the café, but Barker had gone.

"Urgent work call," Evelyn announced as she turned over a tarot card. "*The Ten of Swords*! Oh dear, Julia! I suspect that whatever he wanted to tell you wasn't good. The cards have spoken and something untoward is coming your way."

Julia smiled at the eccentric B&B owner as her mind began to wonder what Barker had been trying to talk to her about. She made a promise that the next time he reached into that inside pocket, she would pay close attention.

CHAPTER 9

After closing the café and squeezing in a spot of Christmas shopping at the out of town retail centre with Jessie, Julia found herself wrapping up the results of her spending on the sitting room floor.

She took a sip of wine, her finger holding the wrapping paper together over the twin pack of socks for Sue's husband, Neil. She ripped off a small piece of tape, secured the paper in place, spun it around, and folded in the edges before taping them down. She had never thought socks were an adequate gift, but according to Sue, Neil was in desperate need of new socks because he did not have a matching pair in his collection. After writing the tag, Julia popped it under the tree with the baby clothes she had bought for Sue's twins.

Leaning into the crackling fire, Julia sipped more of her wine as the Christmas music station played on the TV. Barker was in the dining room, tapping away on the typewriter while he worked on his debut crime novel. She was waiting for her Christmas spirit to kick in, but as long as her gran was behind bars, she was not sure it was ever going to happen. She leaned across to the coffee table she had pushed out of the way earlier, grabbing her mother's photo album, which she had hidden between two magazines. She flicked through the pages, landing on another picture of her parents' wedding, this time with all four of her grandparents.

Her mothers' parents, Frederick and Barbara Dixon stood on her mother's side, grinning at the camera. Frederick died before Julia was born, and Barbara died when she was a baby, so she had no memory of either of them, but her mother had always painted a lovely picture of them. They were much older than her father's parents, having had their only daughter, Pearl, in their forties. On her father's side stood Dot, looking much like the woman outside the court from the front of *The Peridale Post*, her arm looped around Albert. From looking at this picture as a little girl, Julia had regretted not knowing Grandpa Albert the most. Even through the picture, he looked so jolly and happy.

"What are you looking at?" Barker's voice asked from behind the couch, startling Julia.

Out of habit, she snapped the album shut as he threw a cushion on the floor to sit next to her. For a moment, they sat in silence staring into the fire before Julia opened up the book.

"My parents," Julia said, passing him the photograph of her mother and father. "It would have been my mother's sixty-fourth birthday on Christmas day."

"She was a Christmas baby?" Barker said, accepting the album before flicking through some of the pictures. "She was so beautiful. You look just like her."

"I do?"

"You could be her sister." Barker held up her

picture to Julia's face. "Spitting image. I was never sure if I should ask about her, or if I should wait for you to open up."

"I was a little girl when she died," Julia said, the words catching in her throat. "Christmas has always been a weird time for me since then. We'd always have Christmas dinner, open the presents, and then we'd reset the day and pretend it wasn't Christmas, and it was just Mum's birthday. Dad would make bacon sandwiches, even though we were stuffed, and then we'd play party games, and move all the furniture out of the way and dance until we felt sick. When we'd had cake, we'd resume Christmas, and sit in front of the TV playing board games until Gran fell asleep in her chair in the corner."

"Sounds a lot like my family," Barker said with a laugh. "Growing up with all those brothers meant Christmas Day was hectic, to say the least. Mum always got us exactly what we wanted. I don't know how she did it. We never asked, she just read our minds. It's like she spent all year watching and waiting for us to show interest in something and then she'd make a note and save up for it for Christmas. I remember watching '*Home Alone 2*' and obsessing over how cool the *Talkboy* was, and lo and behold, there was one under the tree on Christmas

Day in 1992."

"I wish I could have met your mum."

"Likewise," Barker said as he flicked through the album. "If she was anything like you, I imagine she was an extraordinary woman."

Julia nodded that she was, but the truth was, her memories were sparse and faded now. She could remember snippets of time and smells more than specific details. She accepted the photo album back and replaced it in between the magazines before reaching out for a pair of slippers she had bought for her gran.

"How's the book coming along?" Julia asked as she peeled the price sticker off the bottom of the slippers. "And more importantly, when can I read it?"

"Soon," he said with a mysterious smile. "And I think I'm almost done. A couple more chapters, and then I guess I'm finished. I'm going with the working title of *The Girl in the Basement*, but I need to run that past Evelyn first."

"How did she take you writing a book based on her daughter's body being found under my café after twenty years?" Julia asked as she folded the paper around the slippers. "She didn't seem to want to kill you in the café today."

"She was surprisingly okay with it," Barker said as he stood up. "In fact, she claimed to have foreseen it, so I think that got me some extra points. She thinks it's a great idea that Astrid lives on in my book. I said I wouldn't do anything with it until she had a chance to read it."

"As long as I can read it first," Julia said with a wink as she ripped off a piece of tape. "I keep trying to find chapters lying around, but you hide them well."

"On purpose." Barker walked over to the couch and let out a yawn. "Imagine if the books take off. Wouldn't that be great?"

"I suppose you need a publishing deal first?" Julia replied, not having given the idea of Barker actually finishing the book much thought. "Or maybe you can publish online? I hear that's a trendy thing to do these days. A woman came into my café who swore her cousin's friend's sister had sold a million books doing it all herself online."

Barker smiled uneasily at Julia for a moment. He rubbed across his jaw, his eyes trained on her as though he was about to share bad news.

"About that –"

Before Barker could finish his sentence, Jessie burst through the door laughing, with Billy right behind her. They slammed the door in its frame, chattering between themselves as though they were the only two people in the world. Jessie kicked off her Doc Martens and jumped over the couch, landing in the middle with a thud. She tossed her head back on the couch and let out an exhausted sounding laugh.

"How was ice skating?" Julia asked as she attached a pre-written tag to Dot's gift. "You look like you had fun."

"It was hilarious, Miss S," Billy said as he joined Jessie on the couch. "You two should have come. It was proper top quality."

"I'm sorry we missed out on the '*proper top quality*' fun," Barker said, winking over the couch at Julia before mouthing '*I'll leave you to it*'.

Barker retreated back to the dining room, the tapping of his typewriter keys floating through seconds later. Julia listened to Jessie and Billy recount every fall and stumble on the ice while she finished wrapping the presents. By the time they were all under the tree, Billy and Jessie had decided to walk to the takeaway chicken shop out of the village, leaving Julia and Barker alone again. She walked to the dining room with every intention of asking him what he had been about to tell her, but he looked so deep in thought as his fingers pounded down on the keys, his tongue poking out the side of his mouth, she did not want to disturb him. She knew how irritating it could be to be in the middle of a complicated recipe that required a lot of deep concentration only to be interrupted in the middle of weighing out the rare and expensive ingredient she had spent days tracking down online.

Leaving Barker to his book, Julia walked back into the sitting room, her handbag catching her eye. She pulled out the file of papers Johnny had given her before flicking through them, paying close attention to each of the wedding pictures. After a quick look at the clock, Julia looked at her car keys on the coffee table, deciding how she was going to spend the remainder of the evening.

She scribbled a quick note saying that she was dropping the gifts off at Sue's, stuck the note to the front door, pulled on her pink pea coat and yellow scarf, and jumped into her tiny car.

***

JULIA PULLED UP OUTSIDE THE VILLAGE hall, knowing she had spontaneously decided to arrive at the right time. She jumped out of her car, just as thunderous applause poured out of the hall. She decided to hang back in the dark shadows of St. Peter's Church until the last of the spectators had filtered out of the building.

"I almost expected another real shooting," one woman said.

"I couldn't rest until that boy playing Jimmy Monroe came out for the final curtain," another said. "I was a shivering wreck."

When Julia was satisfied only the cast and crew remained in the village hall, she ditched her coat and scarf but kept Johnny's file rolled up in her back pocket, and slipped inside, thankfully unseen. The crew, along with Jayesh and Poppy, were stacking up the chairs and pushing them to the side of the room. Without taking a second to think about it, Julia hurried down the side of the hall and began stacking up the front row of seats.

"Hurry up!" Carlton's quivering voice cried from the back of the hall. "I need to mop! So many footprints. Always *footprints*!"

Julia gathered up as many chairs as she could and took them to the side of the hall. Not wanting to miss her opportunity, she slipped backstage. Ross' door was open, and he was enjoying a glass of champagne as he sat back in his chair, his eyes closed, clearly exhausted by the stress of having to relaunch the play with a reshuffled cast.

She walked over to the two dressing rooms. Marcus' star had been removed, but Catherine's was still there. The moving shadow in the slither of light under the door let Julia know she had picked her moment perfectly. She pulled the file from her back pocket, flattening it out before looking at the wedding photos again. She quickly turned on her phone's recording feature, pushed it back into her pocket, and decided against knocking.

"*Oh!*" Catherine cried, clearly startled by Julia. "What are you doing? I asked to be left alone."

Catherine had already changed out of her character's costume and was wearing a white silk dressing gown. She had a thick layer of white cream on her face, which she was liberally applying to her hands and arms as she stared at Julia.

"Do you remember me?" Julia asked, closing the door behind her and leaning against it so Catherine could not make a bid for freedom. "Dot is my gran, and is currently in prison for shooting your husband."

Catherine stared at Julia with mild curiosity as she took a seat at her dressing table. She began to brush out her bright blonde hair, the dark roots on top giving away that it was not natural.

"What do you want?" Catherine asked with a huff. "Your family has already put me through enough. That gran of yours has left me a widow."

Julia opened the file, pulled out the wedding photos, and dropped them onto the dressing table in front of Catherine.

"Not for the first time," Julia said firmly, catching Catherine's eyes in the mirror before she looked down at the pictures in front of her. "Recognise yourself? It's rather impressive how much changing your hair colour can change your face."

Catherine flicked through the pictures at arms-length, squinting as though her eyesight was not the best. When she had been through them once, she dropped them back down and shrugged.

"I've never seen those women before in my life," Catherine said, the wobble in her voice betraying her. "What do you want from me?"

"The truth," Julia said as she took the photographs back. "My gran is currently locked up because someone switched the guns. If I don't uncover the truth soon, she'll stay there and likely be convicted at trial."

"And you're suggesting that *I* murdered my husband?" Catherine cried, turning around in her seat. "*Why* on Earth would I want to do *that*?"

"For his money," Julia suggested. "Although I don't know why you'd need it. You did okay out of your last three husbands."

Catherine's eyes seethed, burning holes into Julia's skin. For a brief moment, Julia expected the widow to launch across the dressing room to strangle the life out of her. Instead, she just stared, the muscles in her jaw twitching under the cream.

"They all died of natural causes," Catherine said suddenly, her spine stiffening. "I had nothing to do with their deaths."

"Although, I expect you targeted them because of their poor health?" Julia said, taking a brave step away from the safety of the door. "The unhealthy diabetic in his sixties, the surgery addict with the bad lungs, the old man with cancer, and then Marcus? What was wrong with him?"

"I *beg* your pardon!" Catherine spluttered, letting Julia know nobody had dared be so frank with her. "Get out of here, you little witch!"

"When you met Marcus on holiday, did he tell you about an illness as well as his wealth?" Julia said, holding her ground. "Or was he perfectly healthy, and that's why you switched the guns?"

"I did no such thing!" Catherine screeched,

jumping up and knocking her chair over. "Now get out, before I call the police and have you in the cell next to your precious gran for harassment and slander!"

Julia took a step back, her hands shaking. She clung to the file harder and swallowed her fear down.

"I know you requested the will reading be brought forward," Julia said. "Are you planning a quick exit tomorrow after you hear what you get? Is Ross going to have to recast your part again?"

To Julia's complete surprise, her fear of Catherine launching at her came true very quickly. The widow charged across the room, pinning Julia to the door with her arm against her throat while staring deep into her eyes, her nostrils flared, and teeth bared.

"Listen here, you little snoop," Catherine sneered, her voice deepening. "You won't stand in my way. I am *entitled* to every penny of that pig's money, and I'm going to take it, and get on the first plane to whatever place I feel like. I'm thinking somewhere beginning with B. Barbados? Bulgaria? Boston? Who knows?" Catherine readjusted her arm to push down even harder on Julia's windpipe. "You're not going to do anything about it because I haven't committed any crimes. It's not illegal to inherit a man's fortune. I worked hard for it. Do you know how difficult it was lying down next to that fat slob every night? Now, you're going to walk out of that door, and you're going to keep your nose out, okay?"

Julia did not say a word, not that she could have if she wanted to. She stared deep into Catherine's eyes as she struggled to breathe through her nose.

"Do you understand me?" Catherine cried, pushing down even harder. "Don't make this more difficult than it needs to be."

Julia simply nodded her understanding, which was all Catherine needed to let go. She snatched the file from Julia's hands, and before Julia could register what was happening, she was watching the papers burn in the waste paper basket. Catherine picked up her chair, sat down, lit a cigarette, and watched the fire burn, her back to Julia.

"Close the door on your way out," Catherine mumbled out of the corner of her mouth before blowing up a cloud of grey smoke.

Unsure of what had just happened, Julia stumbled out of the dressing room, closing the door behind her. She pulled her phone from her pocket, glad it had recorded everything. She did not have a confession to murder, but she had a confession to everything Johnny had suspected, so that was something. She also had enough evidence to probably have Catherine charged with assault and threatening behaviour if she wanted to, but that was not Julia's style. If she wanted to get her gran out by Christmas, she needed to play a smarter game.

Rubbing her throat, Julia walked out of the hall, not caring about Carlton mumbling behind her as she made footprints on his freshly mopped floor. Once outside, Julia grabbed her scarf and coat from where she had thrown them on a bench, before sitting on it for a moment. As snow continued to sprinkle down on Peridale, she stared ahead at the village green in a mixture of shock and surprise.

After several minutes had passed, Julia finally stood up and set off to her car, still in somewhat of a daze. She was so distracted by what had just happened that she did not see Poppy sitting on the wall outside the church until she had her key in the car door. Julia pulled it out and turned back to the young woman, whose red hair shone brightly against the white snow as it fell around her. She was looking down at her feet as though she was somewhere else entirely.

"It's cold out tonight," Julia said calmly as she

walked towards the girl. "Do you want me to drop you off somewhere?"

"I'm waiting for my mum," Poppy said, startled by Julia's arrival. "Thank you, though."

Julia took the thanks as an invitation to sit down. She had been desperate to talk properly to the girl since what she had witnessed in the dressing room between her and Marcus. With Poppy's mother seemingly on the way, she knew they probably did not have long.

"When I was seventeen I met a boy at a party," Julia started. "Stanley Kray. He was drunk, and he tried to kiss me. I told him not to, but he didn't seem to understand until my best friend, Roxy, punched him in the nose. You know it's not your fault if things like that happen."

"Okay?" Poppy said, staring at Julia with an arched brow, reminding her of Jessie. "Why are you telling me this?"

"Because I saw what happened in the dressing room when you ran out crying before opening night," Julia said, resting her hand on Poppy's knee. "And it's okay to talk about it."

A red car pulled into the village and drove around the green towards them, the headlights blinding them. Poppy jumped up, her brows tensed hard over her eyes.

"I've got to go," she said, unable to look at Julia. "Bye."

Poppy jumped into the passenger seat next to her similarly redheaded mother who looked suspiciously at Julia before driving away.

"Poor girl," Julia whispered to herself as she climbed into her own car. "Poor, poor girl."

When Julia snuck back into her cottage, her note had gone unnoticed, and Barker did not seem to have moved from his typewriter at the dining room table. Julia silently snuck in with a fresh cup of black coffee before curling up on the couch in front of the fire while '*The Muppet Christmas Carol*' played quietly on the television.

CHAPTER 10

The next morning, Julia drove into the village to see that the travelling Christmas market, which made its way around the Cotswold villages in the run-up to Christmas, had pitched up on the village green. When Julia opened her café, it seemed she was the only person who had not known the market was coming today. Christmas market day was always a busy day for the café, and she usually made sure to bake extra cakes and be fully stocked on all drinks, but she had been so distracted by everything that had been happening, she had not been tuned to the same frequency as the rest of the village.

"Oh, I do love this time of year," Shilpa announced as she sipped a hot chocolate by the counter. "I know I don't *technically* celebrate Christmas, but there is something so magical about the whole thing."

"I have to agree," Evelyn said as she stared out of the window, transfixed by a candle making demonstration on one of the stalls. "I usually spend my winter under a foreign sun, but now that I have a grandson, I thought I'd experience a Peridale Christmas, and I must say I have quite enjoyed it. The snow, the music, the movies on TV, the food, the drinks. It really *is* the most wonderful time of year."

Julia attempted to smile as she stared out of the window at the hundreds of people milling around the market. She looked at the door, half-expecting her gran to burst in any second to say something outrageous about the crowds being a nuisance. It had taken Dot going away for Julia to realise how much her interruptions had become part of her day.

A flash of red hair caught Julia's eye as a snuggly wrapped up Poppy walked past the candle making demonstration, Jayesh on her arm. Julia and Shilpa shared a look before they both watched the young adults walk to a German biscuit stall. Poppy picked something out before Jayesh handed over some money. He fed the young redhead something, making her toss her head back and laugh. It struck Julia that it was the first time she had seen the young woman even smile.

"She is a beautiful girl," Shilpa said as she hugged her mug of hot chocolate. "But there is so much sadness in her heart. And besides, a girl like her will *never* work with my son."

"A girl like her?" Evelyn asked, looking more than a little confused. "You mean a white girl?"

"No!" Shilpa cried, throwing her hands up to the ceiling. "*Ginger*! Imagine the babies. My skin with *that* hair. It's a culture clash no one is asking for, but by all the spices in India, Jayesh seems besotted with her."

The three women laughed as they watched the lovebirds wander deeper into the market. Julia knew what she had witnessed between Marcus and Poppy, and it was probably not the only time the old man had pushed himself on the girl. She wondered if

Poppy had shared this information with her new boyfriend, making her unable to look at Shilpa. She was more than aware that it would implicate the post office owner's son, making him a potential suspect along with Poppy. As she caught a glimpse of the couple looking at a stall of hand-carved Christmas ornaments, she could not bring herself to imagine either of them plotting something so cruel and framing Dot in the process; even if it was just for today, they looked so carefree and in love.

"I must go," Shilpa said as she stood up, throwing her red sari across her shoulder. "My lunch breaks are getting longer and longer, and I put all of the blame on you, Julia South. Your festive menu is quite something. Pass my love onto your grandmother for me."

Julia promised that she would, touched that Shilpa had dropped Dot into the conversation. It had been five days since the shooting, but as usual with Peridale, it seemed the gossip train had moved onto a new topic, leaving Dot at the bottom of the pile until further developments arose. Julia felt the pressure to bring out those further developments, especially since there were only six days until Christmas Day.

"I'm sick of seeing festive themed nonsense,"

Jessie said as she brought a freshly cooked pile of Christmas tree shaped gingerbread biscuits from the kitchen. "All of this for one day."

"Your aura seems tense," Evelyn exclaimed as she fiddled with the crystal around her neck. "Why don't you drop by the B&B later? I'd be more than happy to perform Reiki on you."

Jessie looked down her nose at Evelyn in a way only she could. Julia stifled a laugh.

"I don't know what *that* is, but it sounds cult-y," Jessie said with a shake of her head. "I'll pass."

"Then I'll ask the universe to send you positive vibes," Evelyn said with a soft smile, unaffected by Jessie's sharp tongue. "All the answers you seek are already within you."

Jessie pouted and rolled her eyes as she stacked up the biscuits in the display case. Julia thought about her gran. Were the answers she sought for Dot's freedom already within Julia? Had she heard something, or already discovered the crucial clue to unpicking the stitching of the mystery? She sipped her hot peppermint and liquorice tea, sure that if she had the information already, it had yet to be framed in a light clear enough for her to put together the pieces of the puzzle.

After finishing her apple turnover, Evelyn

floated out of the café, claiming she was going to the graveyard to channel spirits to wish them all a Merry Christmas. She was immediately replaced with a group of chatty women who seemed to be visiting the village for the Christmas market. Leaving Jessie to serve them, Julia began clearing up the tables. She peered out of the window, spotting Poppy and Jayesh sitting on wooden stools drinking hot mulled wine at a makeshift bar; they did not seem to have a care in the world.

When Julia returned from the kitchen with a cloth and surface spray to wipe down the tables, her eyes homed in on a figure marching towards the market. If everyone else had not been lazily wandering from stall to stall in their scarves and woolly hats, Julia might not have seen Catherine speeding like a bullet train, the fury of a thousand scorned women consuming her expression. Unlike the rest of the shoppers, she was inappropriately dressed in a black skirt and jacket, a small fascinator balancing on her head, a mesh veil covering one half of her face. She hurried onto the village green, her heels sinking into the frosty grass. Julia sprayed the table as she watched Catherine march around the stalls, clearly looking for someone. When she spotted Poppy and Jayesh chatting as they cupped their mulled wine, her pace increased, and her expression twisted into the one Julia had seen when Catherine had pinned her to the door the previous night.

Julia dropped the bottle and cloth before heading for the door. As though she could sense what was coming, she made her way towards the young couple, the cold nipping at her exposed arms and legs poking out of her festive red and white flared dress.

"*You*!" Catherine cried, her finger extended at Poppy. "I'm going to *kill* you! How did you do it, you little *witch*?"

Poppy turned around, clearly startled by Catherine's sudden appearance. She stood up, the mulled wine falling from her hands. She stumbled backwards behind Jayesh, who puffed out his chest, blocking Catherine, but her rage seemed to know no bounds. She pushed Jayesh out of the way as though he weighed no more than a crunchy fallen leaf. Poppy walked backwards away from the advancing woman, but she was too slow. Both of Catherine's fists grabbed Poppy's red hair before swinging her around like a dog toy. The market suddenly stopped, the happy chatter replaced with gasps, but no one rushed forward to help Poppy.

"How did you do it?" Catherine cried as she

rattled Poppy. "*How*? I'm going to *kill* you!"

Julia snapped to her senses, rushing forward into the fray. She grabbed at Catherine's jacket, but her hands were clamped to Poppy's hair like a shark biting into its prey.

"Get off her!" Jayesh screamed, joining Julia in trying to pull Catherine off the whimpering girl. "Have you lost your mind?"

"No, but *she* has!" Catherine cried. "She's stolen *my* fortune!"

Julia remembered something Barker had once told her about self-defence techniques. She nipped hard under both of Catherine's arms, causing the woman to scream. She released Poppy before spinning around, the back of her hand striking Julia's face. She felt the rough surface of Catherine's diamond wedding ring cut across her lip as she stumbled back.

The gasping crowd was replaced with a tribal scream as a second figure dressed all in black launched across the village green. Julia did not realise what was happening until she saw Jessie fly on top of Catherine, tackling her like an experienced rugby player into the mud. Everyone screamed and gasped, jumping back as the savage teenager pinned the manic woman into the mud.

"How *dare* you hit her!" Jessie cried, her eyes filled with rage as she shook the lapels of Catherine's jacket. "How *dare* you!"

Cupping her bleeding lip, Julia hurried forward, pulling Jessie off Catherine just as her fist raised in the air. Jessie reluctantly gave in, letting Julia drag her back. Poppy hid again behind Jayesh, the confusion across her face letting Julia know she had no idea why Catherine had suddenly attacked.

"What is going on here?" Julia cried, putting her hands between Jessie and Catherine when the widow had staggered to her feet. "You're a fully-grown woman, Catherine. Poppy is a teenager."

"She knew *exactly* what she was doing!" Catherine cried, bumping into Julia, but not trying too hard to get past her. "I've just come from the will reading, and my beloved *idiot* of a husband has left that little *witch* every penny! *Every last penny*! How did you do it, *huh*? Did you flutter your eyelashes and flash a bit of leg?"

Julia opened her mouth to speak as she turned to Poppy, but no words came out. Jayesh stood his ground protecting Poppy, but even he seemed confused. Poppy looked down at the ground before bursting into tears. Without waiting another second, she ran off, closely followed by Jayesh.

"That's *right*!" Catherine cried as she straightened up the fascinator balancing on her blonde curls. "*Run!* You've just made yourself a *very* rich little girl!"

"I think you should go," Julia said, holding up a hand to Catherine. "For your own sake."

Catherine dusted down her jacket as she looked around the watching crowd, her eyes showing her sudden realisation of where she was and what she had just done. She wobbled on her heels for a moment before turning and heading back the way she had come.

"Isn't that her from the play?" a woman in the crowd whispered.

"She's probably grief stricken!" another announced. "Poor thing."

"Who was that redheaded girl?" another cried. "What did she do?"

Leaving the crowd to erupt into a flurry of gossip, Julia walked back to the café with Jessie, which had emptied. Julia twisted the lock, flipped the sign, and walked into the kitchen.

"I could have killed her," Jessie whispered as she dabbed at Julia's cut lip with a cold cloth. "I wanted to. I've never felt so protective of a person before."

Julia tried to smile, but winced instead as Jessie

pressed down on the cloth.

"I appreciate you having my back," Julia said. "But maybe next time, we keep the public assaults to a minimum, okay?"

Jessie smirked as she grabbed the first aid kit from on top of the fridge. She pulled out the antiseptic spray before spraying it on Julia's lip without warning. She cried out, knowing it was for the best, but wincing nonetheless. Jessie then applied a small plaster before telling her she was done.

"You know I'd do anything for you," Jessie said, reaching up to the fridge to put the kit back. "Adoption certificate or not, you're still my mum."

Julia's heart swelled in her chest, the pain vanishing from her lip for a moment. She pulled Jessie into a hug, and the two women stayed there for what felt like a lifetime. So much had changed since that first night Julia had caught Jessie stealing cakes from her café at the beginning of the year; she could hardly believe it was the same girl.

"We're going to get that certificate," Julia said when she finally pulled away, Jessie's face cupped in her palms. "Even if we have to kick open every door and fight until the end. We *will* make it official."

Jessie nodded, and for a moment, she seemed to believe and trust Julia without question. They both jumped when knuckles rattled the glass of the café door. Julia headed through the beads and squinted at Barker as he cupped his hands against the glass.

"What just happened?" Barker asked, his eyes drifting to the plaster on Julia's lip. "Are you alright? We just had half a dozen calls about a fight."

"I'm fine," Julia said, looping her arm around Jessie's shoulder when she joined her in the café. "Jessie handled it."

Barker looked down at them both, his eyes clearly full of questions. Instead of asking, he simply wrapped his arms around them, and the three of them hugged each other. Julia peered over his shoulder at the Christmas market as uniformed officers in high visibility yellow jackets walked from person to person.

Julia's mind wandered to Poppy as Barker's clean aftershave tickled her nostrils. Poppy had looked surprised to hear that she inherited Marcus' fortune, but two questions were burning in Julia's mind: how, and more importantly, why?

CHAPTER 11

"Marcus left his money to *Poppy*?" Dot cried down the phone. "But that makes *no* sense!"

"I know," Julia mumbled through a mouthful of hot, buttery toast, the early morning winter sun blinding her through the kitchen window. "Maybe he felt guilty for trying to seduce Poppy, so he wrote her into his will?"

"That *quickly*?" Dot mumbled, the cogs in her brain echoing down the phone as she tried to figure it out. "And with what you told me about Catherine, surely she made sure that Marcus had written *her* into his will? It would make more sense if Marcus had left everything to Ross, but *Poppy*? It's so random."

Before Julia could ask how prison was treating her, a warning message beeped to let them know they only had a minute left, not that Dot used it. She told Julia she needed to grab some breakfast because she was going to a Christmas card crafting class. After she hung up, Julia sat at her kitchen counter, the reams and reams of notes she had made in front of her. She had written pages and pages about Catherine, repeating most of what she had read in the destroyed file from memory. She had as many notes about Marcus and his history with her gran. She had a page written about Ross' shake up of the Peridale Amateur Dramatics Society, a page about Jayesh being protective of his girlfriend, and a single question mark on a page labelled '*Poppy*'.

"You're up early," Barker whispered as he kissed her on the top of her head. "Is there any bread left for toast? The smell is making my stomach rumble."

Julia nodded at the bread bin as she sipped her

peppermint and liquorice tea. She almost choked when she registered that Barker was wearing a Santa Claus costume, complete with the beard. She watched as he dropped two pieces of bread into the toaster, waiting for an explanation.

"We're volunteering at the children's hospital this morning," Barker said, finally turning around with a hot cup of coffee in his hand. He pulled the white beard down and let it hang around his neck. "Believe it or not, I pulled the long straw. The rest of them are either elves or reindeer."

"It suits you," Julia said with a smirk. "Brings out the red in your cheeks."

Jessie stumbled out of her bedroom, her hair matted and her eyes half closed. She let out a long yawn as she walked over to the kettle. After plopping a peppermint and liquorice teabag into a cup, she grabbed the toast when it popped out of the toaster before slathering it in butter.

"I guess I'll grab something on the way in," Barker said with a scowl while Jessie munched on the toast as she waited for the kettle to boil.

"You're five days early," Jessie said as she licked the butter from her lips before poking Barker's padded stomach. "Can you still fit down the chimney?"

"Very funny," Barker said before ducking in to kiss Julia. He hovered there for a moment, resting his finger on the healing cut on her lips. "I don't think it will scar. You know you can still press charges."

"And implicate Jessie?" Julia replied with a shake of her head. "The only thing stopping Catherine running to the police is that she did the exact same to Poppy."

"Well, the results for the fingerprint we found on the gun should be in today," Barker said before gulping down the rest of his coffee. "So, who knows? Maybe we'll be bringing her in after all."

With a final kiss on Julia's head, Barker headed for the door, leaving them alone in the kitchen. Jessie finished her toast, still not looking like she had woken up yet. After a slurp of hot tea, she stretched, letting out a long yawn, almost unhinging her jaw.

"What needs baking?" she asked as she scratched under her arm. "There wasn't much left in the café after that Christmas market yesterday."

"All done," Julia said, nodding to the fridge. "I pulled out one of my Christmas cakes. It's been maturing nicely since September."

"Ew," Jessie said with a wrinkled nose as she checked in the fridge. "That's gross. In that case, I'm going for a long, long shower."

With joints as stiff as an old woman, Jessie plodded off to the bathroom, leaving Julia to look over her notes again. She picked up the page she had written about the event at the Christmas market the previous day. As she listened to the sound of running water and Jessie's out of tune singing, Julia continued to try and figure out why Marcus would leave his inheritance to Poppy.

Her thoughts were broken when the sound of shattering glass echoed through her silent cottage. At first, she thought Mowgli might have knocked something over in the sitting room until he popped his head out of the bedroom to see where the noise had come from.

"What was that?" Jessie called from the bathroom. "Are you alright?"

Leaving her notes, Julia slid off the stool and walked slowly into the sitting room. Her heart sank when she saw the shattered window pane next to her Christmas tree.

"What the –" she whispered as she bent down to pick up a small rock, a paper note wrapped around it in string like a badly wrapped Christmas gift. "Jessie, stay where you are!"

With the rock in her hand, Julia hurried to the

front door, still in her reindeer pyjamas. She stepped onto her doorstep, the cold stone stinging her feet. Looking up and down the quiet winding lane, she knew whoever had thrown the rock had already vanished. Craning her neck, Julia looked at the missing glass in her window, knowing it must have taken some force to throw the small stone all the way from the other side of the garden wall.

"What the *hell*?" Jessie cried from behind Julia, a towel around her chest as she dripped water on the floorboards. "Who did that?"

Julia closed the front door and nodded to the rock in her hands. She carefully unwrapped the string, letting the stiff paper bounce away from the stone. She turned it over, the giant red letters making her heart sink.

"'*STAY AWAY*'," Julia read aloud. "'*OR YOU'LL BE NEXT*'."

"Someone is threatening you?" Jessie cried as her teeth began to chatter. "I'll kill them! What are we going to do?"

"We're going straight to the police," Julia said, putting the rock and paper on the side table, eager not to add any more fingerprints to it. "This finally proves that someone else is behind all of this."

***

"THIS DOESN'T PROVE ANYTHING," DS John Christie said as he dropped the note onto the interview table. "It's too vague."

"Too *vague?*" Julia echoed, stabbing her finger down on the red writing. "It says right there '*YOU'LL BE NEXT*'. Do I need to be dead for this to be serious?"

DS Christie was a colleague of Barker's with whom Julia had dealt before during the events surrounding Barker's birthday the previous month; he had been dismissive of her thoughts then too.

"It is serious," DS Christie said as he leaned back in his chair before tugging at the tie around his neck. "But it doesn't prove that it's connected to *this* murder case. You get around, Julia. How many people have you annoyed this year? I bet half the village want to kill you for getting involved in all of the murder cases you have."

"And correctly solved," Julia reminded him with a frown. "And I don't '*get involved*' unless there is a reason. My gran is behind bars for something she didn't do."

"She *did* shoot and kill a man."

"But she didn't know she was going to," Julia corrected him, joining DS Christie and falling back into her own chair. "And you wonder why I've solved so many cases *without* your help? You can't look far enough past the end of your nose to see what's right in front of you."

DS Christie stared across the table at Julia, his jaw gritted tightly. She knew she was likely a couple of words away from getting herself locked up in a cell, but she was not sure that she cared much for her own freedom anymore if the person who switched the gun was onto her.

"I'll get the boys to look into it," he said before walking over to the door to hold it open for Julia. "Just stay out of trouble, and call us if anything else happens."

Leaving the note behind, Julia walked out of the station and took her phone from her pocket. She pulled up the picture she had taken of the note while she was still at her cottage. She stared at it for the longest time outside the station in the hope she would recognise something about the handwriting, but it seemed to have been intentionally written in indistinguishable block capital letters. Tucking the phone back into her pocket, Julia headed towards her café where Jessie was already working. As she walked past the village green, which was now empty thanks to the Christmas market already having moved on, she looked over at her gran's empty cottage on the other side. She let out a sigh, guilt consuming her for not having put the pieces together yet.

"*Julia*?" a voice cried across the village.

Julia turned towards the church where Shilpa was running towards her, barely recognisable in a pair of jeans and a loose kaftan shirt instead of her usual ornamental sari. Julia did not need to be right in front of Shilpa to feel the worry radiating from her.

"What's wrong?" Julia called as she ran to meet Shilpa halfway across the green, the early morning frost still hard underfoot. "Has something happened?"

"It's Jayesh!" Shilpa cried, her hands disappearing up into her hair, her face completely makeup free and her eyes lacking her usual dark eyeliner. "He's *gone*!"

"Gone?" Julia echoed. "What do you mean?"

"I just checked his room to take him in a cup of tea, and he wasn't there," Shilpa cried, her hand resting on her forehead as she looked around the quiet village. "All his clothes are gone, and he's not answering his phone."

Julia joined Shilpa in looking helplessly around

the village for a moment as she tried to think logically about what she was hearing.

"Where have you checked?" Julia asked, resting both hands on Shilpa's shoulders. "Someone will have seen him."

"The village hall is locked up," Shilpa said, her voice trembling. "I thought he might have gone for an early morning rehearsal. His father is driving around the country lanes looking for him. What if he's run away and I never see him again?"

"That's not going to happen," Julia said reassuringly as she looked back at her car, which was parked between her café and Shilpa's post office. "Let's drive around and look. If it takes all day, it takes all day."

Shilpa stared blankly at Julia for a moment as though the words had not sunk in. Julia gave her shoulders a firm squeeze, prompting Shilpa to nod her head. Arm in arm, the two women set off to Julia's car.

"Julia?" Jessie called from the bottom of the narrow alley after hefting a black bag into the large bin. "Everything alright?"

"Jayesh is missing," Shilpa said as she climbed into the car. "He vanished this morning."

"I just saw him," Jessie said, looking down the

country path that ran behind the café. "With Poppy. They just walked down here about ten minutes ago."

"They did?" Shilpa cried, half out of the car. "Where were they going?"

"I dunno," Jessie said with a shrug. "I was just emptying the mop bucket. They had huge bags though. Looked like they were going somewhere."

"Have you checked the train station?" Julia asked over the roof of the car. Shilpa shook her head, prompting them both to quickly jump into the car.

CHAPTER 12

Julia gave Jessie a quick wave before reversing out of the alley, her tyres screeching on the icy road. She drove slowly past the police station before immediately speeding up. She took the sharp corners and narrow lanes faster than she had ever dared, even though she did not know for certain they were even heading to the right place. She knew Poppy and Jayesh were planning to run away together; it would be very possible to assume they might never see either of them again, potentially leaving the truth uncovered and trapping Dot behind bars for the years she had left.

"There's a train going to Scotland in two minutes," Shilpa read aloud from her phone. "Jayesh has an old school friend who is at university in Glasgow. Why would he do this?"

"Maybe they have something to hide?" Julia suggested, pushing her foot down onto the accelerator as they flew over a bump in the road. "Something happened between Marcus and Poppy, and he left his entire inheritance to her. His wife wasn't too happy about that, so maybe they're running away from her?"

They drove in silence until they screeched up in front of the train station at the exact minute the train was due to depart. They jumped out of the car and sprinted through the ticket office to the platform, just at the moment the electronic doors shuddered to a close.

"*Damn!*" Shilpa cried as her fists beat down on the door. "We're too late!"

Julia ran along the platform, her eyes glued on the windows. Her heart skipped a beat when she saw the back of a redheaded woman reaching up to put her large bag in the overhead compartment. When she was done, she turned around, and Julia's heart skipped another beat when she locked eyes with Poppy. Behind her, Jayesh was sat at a table, his eyes also glued on Julia.

"They're here!" Julia called as she ran back to Shilpa, not wanting to waste another second. "Come on! The train is stopping at Riverswick next. I think we can beat them."

They doubled back, sprinting through the ticket office again. The second they were back in the car, Julia sped out of the station, almost hitting a little old lady dragging a shopping cart in the process. When they were back on the road, Julia dug into her memory banks to remember the quickest way to Riverswick village. A shortcut she and Sue used to take on their bikes sprang to mind, forcing her to take a sudden sharp left to cut down an old dirt track running alongside a farm.

"At least we know they're safe," Shilpa cried, her voice shaking as the car bounced along the stony road. "That boy hasn't been thinking clearly since Poppy came into his life."

They took another sharp turn back onto a winding country lane. Julia allowed herself to smile when they zoomed past the black and white

'*Welcome to Riverswick village*' sign jutting out from a bush. When the train station came into view at the end of the road, they shared a quick smile.

"I think you were a rally driver in a previous life," Shilpa said, her hands firmly on the dashboard to steady herself as Julia skidded to a halt. "Let's hope that wasn't a waste of time."

As though fate was smiling down on them, a train eased out of a tunnel and onto the platform as they sprinted to the station, which was even smaller than the one in Peridale. Without even checking that it was the right train, they both jumped on when the nearest doors opened. Shilpa stepped forward to press a button to open the doors to the compartment, but Julia pulled her back.

"If they see us, they can jump off, and I don't think we can outrun two teenagers," Julia whispered. "I need to talk to Poppy to find out the truth, and if that means trapping her on a train, that's what I need to do."

Shilpa nodded her understanding. They stood out of view from the carriage, smiling awkwardly at the conductor when she came out of her cabin. Neither of them moved until the doors closed, and the train shuddered into life.

"*The next stop is Cheltenham at nine-twenty,*" a

robotic voice announced, letting Julia know they had at least fifteen minutes on the train whether they were on the right one or not.

Shilpa pressed the button and the internal doors slid open. They walked down the carriage, checking the faces of the passengers in the almost empty train; none of the early morning commuters jumped out at them. Julia gulped as they pressed another set of buttons to take them into another carriage.

They entered a tunnel, blocking out the outside world. The train shuddered, swaying from side to side as it sped up even more. Shilpa grabbed hold of the back of a chair to steady herself, causing the suited man sitting down to scowl up at her. Julia smiled an apology as she passed. Shilpa suddenly ground to a halt at the moment they burst out of the tunnel, the early morning sun blinding them. Shilpa nudged Julia in the side as she nodded down the carriage to a table.

"It's them," Shilpa whispered over her shoulder. "Let's move in slowly."

As the train rattled from side to side, zooming in and out of another short tunnel, they made their way slowly down the carriage towards the table where Jayesh and Poppy were seated, both looking out of the window as the countryside whizzed past.

Without saying a word, Shilpa and Julia took the empty seats next to them, causing them both to spin around.

"What is wrong with you, boy?" Shilpa cried as she slapped Jayesh around the back of the head. "What do you think you're playing at? *Hm*? Running out like that and taking your things. Your father and I were worried sick!"

"*Dammit*, Mum!" Jayesh cried, his cheeks darkening. "Why couldn't you just let us go? I would have called you when we arrived."

"In *Scotland*?" Shilpa cried, slapping him around the back of the head again. "Was I supposed to be okay with my youngest son running away? Was I supposed to be content with a phone call at Diwali and on my birthday? *Stupid* boy! I raised you *better* than this."

"It was my idea," Poppy whispered, her voice small as she looked down at her fingers as she chipped off her red nail polish. "I told Jayesh to stay, but he insisted on coming with me."

"Because I love you," Jayesh said, reaching out to grab her hands. "I wouldn't let you go alone."

"By the arms of Shiva, boy!" Shilpa muttered as she planted her face in her hands. "Children do stupid things in the name of love."

"I'm *nineteen*!" Jayesh cried, his brows tensing over his eyes, similar to a look Jessie liked to pull. "And it's no different than my dad. You ran away because your mum didn't want you to marry him."

"That was different," Shilpa said. "She wanted me to marry a nice Indian boy, but I'd already fallen in love with your father, and my mother wasn't going to stand by while I married a man with Gerald Smith for a name! And people wonder why I kept my father's surname. Shilpa Smith! Sounds like a bad drag queen."

"Exactly," Jayesh said, squeezing Poppy's hands. "You can't help who you fall in love with, Mum. I love Poppy, and I wasn't going to leave her."

Poppy looked at Jayesh in the same way she had at him during the Christmas market before Catherine had attacked. Julia could not help but also smile because their love seemed so pure, even if there was a hint of sadness in Poppy's eyes.

"Why are you running away, Poppy?" Julia asked calmly, turning in her seat to face the young woman. "It only makes you look like you've done something wrong."

"But if I stay, I have to live with the stares of people looking at me wondering why Marcus left me everything," Poppy said. "And it makes it look like *I* switched the gun, and I swear on my mum's life that I didn't."

"I wouldn't blame you if you did," Julia whispered. "After what he did to you, no one would blame you."

Poppy frowned at Julia for a moment before looking at Jayesh who looked just as confused.

"But he didn't know," Poppy said. "Not until I joined the club as part of my college course."

"Didn't know what?" Julia asked, looking at Shilpa who could only offer a shrug. "I saw you in his dressing room. I saw him brush your hair and make you cry. You don't have to keep his secret. I know it's difficult to talk about, but if you told people the truth, they'd understand. They'd see he left you his money out of guilt."

"It was out of guilt," Poppy said as she reached into her pocket to pull out a folded-up photograph. "But you've got it all wrong. You didn't see what you think you saw. He was my *father*."

Julia and Shilpa both gasped at the same time as Poppy put the photograph on the table between them. Julia stared down at what appeared to be a cast photograph taken outside the village hall in Peridale. Julia spotted Marcus standing in the middle of the picture, a redheaded woman next to him. For a moment, Julia was confused because the woman looked just like Poppy, but Marcus looked younger. She turned the photograph around, glad to see that someone had dated the picture.

"'*The cast of 'Chitty Chitty Bang Bang' – Peridale December 1997*'," Julia read aloud. "Is this your mum?"

Poppy nodded as she took the photograph from Julia. She stared down at the redheaded woman in the picture, who did not look much older than Poppy was now. Marcus, on the other hand, looked to be in his forties.

"I never knew who my dad was growing up," Poppy said, her finger resting on her mother's face. "She never wanted to talk about it. I knew I wasn't like the other kids with two parents, but I stopped asking eventually. She'd get upset and angry. I never expected to find my dad. I never went looking for him, and he couldn't come looking for me because he didn't know I existed."

"Marcus was your father?" Julia asked, the thought still confusing. "When did you find out?"

"About two weeks ago," Poppy said, turning the photograph over to read the caption. "I joined the Peridale Amateur Dramatics Society in September as part of my college course. I was only supposed to be working backstage, but I loved every second of it. As the weeks passed, Marcus started acting stranger and stranger around me. He'd lose his temper at me for no reason, and I didn't understand why he was picking on me. It wasn't until my mum came to pick me up one day that he figured out who I was. Catherine was smoking a cigarette in front of the church, and Marcus was reading over his lines. Mum would never come in, she'd just pull up long enough for me to jump in. She would never tell me why she left the club, and she tried to stop me from going. I think the only reason she let me was because it was part of my education. She wanted me to have a better start than she had."

"So, Marcus figured out that you were his daughter when he saw your mother?" Shilpa asked, her hand drifting up to her mouth. "How did he know?"

"They had an affair during the production of '*Chitty Chitty Bang Bang*'," Poppy said, looking at the cast photograph again. "Marcus played the Child Catcher, and my mum played Truly Scrumptious. Marcus was married to another woman at the time, but I think their relationship was coming to an end. After Christmas, Mum found out she was pregnant. She was scared, so she left the club and moved away.

She told me she'd heard about his prison past and she didn't want to raise a baby around him. Two weeks ago, when Marcus saw my mother, he confronted her the next day when she picked me up, and the truth came out. He'd put the dates together, and he said he'd always wondered why she'd just vanished. He said the reason he'd had a temper with me was because I reminded him so much of my mother, and when he realised that I was his daughter, his attitude completely changed."

"For the better," Jayesh jumped in. "He really wanted to make up for lost time."

Poppy folded up the photograph and tucked it back into her pocket. She stared out of the window for a moment, her mind seeming to be somewhere else entirely.

"You always think there's more time," Poppy whispered without turning back. "You never think you'll find your father and *not* have time to get to know them. I was still adjusting to it. He kept trying to buy me gifts and tried to talk to me, but I wasn't ready to face the truth. The night you saw me in his dressing room, he told me that he had always wanted a daughter. It felt like a blow because I had always wanted a father. I couldn't piece together how I was feeling. I blamed him, but it wasn't his fault. He didn't know."

"And then he was shot," Shilpa said with a shake of her head. "So cruel."

"For two weeks, I had a father," Poppy said as she began to sniffle. "And I spent those two weeks pushing him away. How can I live with myself? I don't *want* his money, I *want* more time."

Poppy melted into Julia's side, so she wrapped her arm around the girl and held her like she would Jessie. How could Julia have got everything so wrong?

"Tickets from Peridale and Riverswick," the conductor announced as she made her way down the carriage. "Any tickets?"

Jayesh pulled his wallet out, but Shilpa rested her hand on his. She pulled her own purse out of her jeans pocket and pulled out two twenty pound notes.

"Four returns from Riverswick to Cheltenham," Shilpa said to the conductor. "Same day."

The woman accepted the money before printing out the tickets. Shilpa tore them out and passed them around.

"We're getting off at the next stop and waiting for the first train to take us back to Julia's car," Shilpa said firmly. "Nothing will be gained from running away. Poppy, I'm sorry you didn't get to know your father like I know you would have wanted to, but we cannot change what has happened. All we can do is look within and work on ourselves to make tomorrow a better day. You cannot blame yourself for the unfortunate turn of events, unless either of you wants to confess to switching those guns."

"I didn't do it," Poppy said, suddenly sitting up and wiping her nose. "I swear I didn't do it."

"Jayesh Patil-Smith?" Shilpa demanded, turning to her son. "Did you switch those guns?"

"*Mum!*" Jayesh exclaimed. "You know I wouldn't do that."

"If you had asked me last night if my son would run away, I would have laughed in your face, but here we are," Shilpa said with a stern look at her son. "But I believe you."

Before the conversation could go any deeper, they pulled into Cheltenham station. After grabbing hot drinks from a small coffee shop, they waited the twenty-five minutes until a train came in the opposite direction. They rode back to Riverswick in a contemplative silence, which was only broken when they were walking back to Julia's messily parked car.

"I didn't know he was leaving his money to me," Poppy said as she crammed her bag into the boot. "I don't want it. I don't deserve it. Catherine was his wife."

"I don't think she deserves it either," Julia said, almost under her breath. "Don't make any rash decisions. He might not have been there for you in your life, but his money might be able to give you a different future than one you might have had otherwise. I'm sure these things take time anyway."

With Shilpa in the front seat and the teenagers in the back, they drove back to Peridale. When Julia passed the police station, and her café came into view, she was relieved by the thought of having some normalcy in her day, even if she still did not know how her discovery of Poppy's connection to Marcus fit into the bigger picture.

They pulled into her space between the café and the post office, and they collectively jumped out.

"How about some breakfast?" Julia suggested as she pulled their bags out of the boot. "On me."

"That sounds like the best idea I've heard all morning," Shilpa said with a laugh. "Jayesh, stay where I can see you."

They walked around the side of the building, and Julia was relieved to see that the café was empty.

She pulled on the door, the little bell above the door ringing out, startling Jessie as she wiped down the cake display cabinet glass.

"*There* she is!" a shrill voice cried across the village. "Don't *move*!"

Julia spun around, and for the second time that week, she saw Catherine running across the village green, this time followed by two uniformed police officers and DS Christie. Julia's heart sank, the urge to jump back in her car to drive away catching her by surprise. It was not until one of the officers grabbed Poppy that Julia realised they had not been running towards her.

"What are you doing?" Julia cried as they handcuffed Poppy. "It's not a crime to inherit. She has a *rightful* claim to that money."

"Poppy Johnston?" DS Christie said as his officer tightened the cuffs behind her back. "I'm arresting you on suspicion of conspiracy to murder."

Julia stood by completely dumbfounded as DS Christie read the bewildered looking girl her rights. She caught Shilpa out of the corner of her eye practically restraining Jayesh as he tried to get at his girlfriend. When DS Christie was finished, Julia stepped forward, her mouth open to speak, but the DS put a finger up, silencing her.

"We had a positive match to a fingerprint we pulled off the gun," he whispered as he passed her. "It belongs to Poppy."

Julia watched in horror as they marched Poppy back to the police car parked outside the village hall. She did not know what to do or say, so she just watched the scene unfold, the world melting away from her.

"But I believed her when she said she didn't do it," Julia whispered. "I *believed* her."

CHAPTER 13

"Maybe it was for revenge," Sue suggested as she dug through the rack of baby clothes in the small boutique on Mulberry Lane. "What do you think about this? Whoever decided that yellow was the gender-neutral colour clearly had no taste."

Sue put the tiny T-shirt back before waddling across the shop to the wall of tiny shoes. She checked the prices on a couple of pairs before putting them straight back, a horrified look on her face.

"But Poppy wanted to get to know her father," Julia said, following Sue across the shop. "She said she was upset that they didn't have more time."

"She could have been lying," Sue said, pausing to rest a hand on her giant bump, clearly exhausted. "Neil said they're the size of watermelons right now, and it feels like it. I can barely breathe."

"I told you not to come out today," Julia said, smiling at the shop assistant as she stared at them. "You could drop *any* day now."

"Exactly," Sue said through gritted teeth as she pushed against her lower back. "I'm going to be trapped in my house for the next eighteen years. I want to enjoy my freedom while I can. Evelyn laid hands on me in the supermarket yesterday. She thinks I'm having two girls."

"What do you think?" Julia asked as she rested a hand on Sue's stomach. "I think it's one of each."

"I think they might *actually* be watermelons," Sue said as she moved Julia's hand across her stomach. "Can you feel that? It's like they're trying to kick their way out."

Sue pressed Julia's hand hard into her stomach until she could feel something solid pushing up against the skin. A small part of her was horrified, but an even bigger part of her was completely fascinated by what was going on inside her sister's body.

"Let's get out of here," Sue said, tucking her hand under her bump. "I need to get off this white carpet. I never know when I'm going to *go*, if you get what I'm talking about. All it takes is a sneeze, and it's *all* over."

Arm in arm they carefully made their way out of the small shop before wandering slowly further down Mulberry Lane, a quaint shopping street in the village, which dated back to the 1700s. Julia pulled out her Christmas list and traced her finger across the items she needed to buy.

"I need something for Jessie," Julia said. "And something for Barker, and then I think I'm done."

"I don't know how you juggle everything," Sue said as they peered at the Christmas display in the window of Pretty Petals. "Between the café, the adoption, Barker, and trying to get Gran out, I'm surprised the men in white coats haven't come for you."

"There's still time," Julia said with a wink as she looked across the street at a small shoe shop. "How about a new pair of Doc Martens for Jessie? She's scuffed hers up pretty bad."

"Perfect. Just get any colour apart from black. That girl is always ready for a funeral."

They walked across the road, the sun setting in the distance behind their father's antique barn at the bottom of the lane. The Christmas lights strung across the street suddenly lit up, and as though to complete the scene, snow began to delicately flutter in the wind.

After seeing a pair of burgundy Doc Martens in the window, they walked into the small shop. The kindly old man smiled at them from behind the counter before looking back at the customer he was serving. When Julia realised it was not just a random shopper, and that it was Ross Miller, the director of the Christmas play, her heart sank a little.

"It's a shame the rest of the shows aren't going ahead," the shopkeeper said as he accepted something from Ross. "I think the wife was really looking forward to seeing it after all the buzz. But I appreciate you personally bringing around a refund for the tickets. Not many would do that."

"I've lost my cast twice now," Ross said with a bitter laugh. "It would be almost impossible to reboot the show for a third time. I'd better go. I have another eighty-three refunds to hand out for tonight's show. Word will hopefully spread and people will come to me for the rest."

Ross turned around, stopping in his tracks when he spotted Julia. For a moment, neither of them seemed to know how to react to each other, so Julia pushed forward a smile and was glad when it was returned.

"I'm sorry to hear about the show," Julia offered, looking down at the clipboard of names and addresses in Ross' hand. "I think you've worked really hard on it."

"Thanks," Ross said, giving Julia a curious look. "Although I suppose you've heard about what happened with Poppy this morning."

"I have," Julia said vaguely. "I heard she's still being questioned by the police."

"I never thought she had it in her to plan something like that," Ross said with a forced laugh. "She always seemed a little wet behind the ears, like she wouldn't say boo to a ghost. It's always the quiet ones, isn't it?"

"Didn't your uncle tell you that he'd left his fortune to Poppy?" Sue asked as she heaved herself down on one of the trying-on benches. "That seems like something an uncle would share with a nephew."

"We weren't particularly close," Ross said with a shrug. "And since Catherine found out about being disinherited, she's refusing to take part in the show. I think she's already booked a flight out of the country. She mentioned something about spending Christmas in Barbados, but I wasn't really listening. I didn't think my uncle had actually changed his will to leave everything to her in the first place, but she seemed sure that he had. Claimed to have sat in on the session with the lawyer. I guess my uncle wasn't as sensible as he seemed, but that's what happens when you're old and dying."

"Dying?" Julia echoed, the word burning in her throat. "Your uncle was dying?"

"According to the autopsy," Ross said with a nod as he glanced down at the list of names. "They said it was late stages of colon cancer. I don't know if he knew or not, but if he did, he kept it quiet. I should get on with these. It's going to be a long night."

Ross walked around Julia and opened the door. Before he left the shop, he turned back to her before pulling a pen from his pocket. He quickly wrote something down on the corner of one of the sheets before tearing it off.

"Now that they've found out it was Poppy, can

you pass this onto your gran when she gets out?" Ross passed Julia the slip of paper containing his phone number. "She's one of the best actresses I've had the pleasure of working with, and I wouldn't mind writing another part for her wherever I end up next."

Julia slipped the paper into her handbag before turning to the display of Doc Martens. She picked out the burgundy pair along with a pair of black ones just to be safe. When she had Jessie's sizes, she took them over to the counter and paid for them. When they left the shop, the sun had completely set, and Sue clearly had something on her mind.

"If Poppy did it, why haven't they let Gran out?" Sue asked as they made their way down the winding lane to the antique barn. "Surely one of us would have heard something from her lawyer by now?"

"Because they have twenty-four hours to charge Poppy and it hasn't even been twelve yet," Julia said after checking her watch. "And we still don't know that she did it. They only have a fingerprint against her, which isn't enough to charge her."

"And her motive," Sue reminded her. "If she *did* know she was going to inherit, it's all they need to cook up a case. I know you believe the girl, but people do lie."

Julia knew Sue had a point, not that she wanted to admit she thought Poppy had lied to her on the train. She had seen how much it had taken to confess the truth about Marcus being the father she would never get the chance to know. If Poppy had lied, she was a better actress than she had portrayed in the role of Mandy Smith.

They walked into the antique barn, which was filled with old pieces of furniture, giant paintings, and displays of coins, stamps, jewellery, and everything in between. Their father was inspecting a collection of medals at the counter, a magnifier clenched in his eye socket.

"*Girls*!" he exclaimed as he popped out the magnifier. "What a lovely surprise. Is there any news about your gran? I heard about that ginger girl being arrested."

"Not yet," Julia said as she looked around the huge barn she had spent so many hours in as a little girl in the years before her mother's death. "I'm actually here to do a spot of shopping. I was looking for something for Barker's Christmas present, and I thought who better to ask than you."

"I have just the thing," Brian said with a click of his fingers. "Wait here."

He scurried off into the depths of his collection. Sue slumped down in an expensive looking chair, her head cupped in her palm as she leaned her elbow against the arm. She looked like she could fall asleep at any moment.

"Do people actually buy this junk?" Sue whispered as she rubbed between her eyes. "None of it looks valuable."

"Value means different things to different people," their father exclaimed as he came back with a dusty book. "A friend of mine pulled that sofa from a skip, not realising it was worth well over four thousand pounds to the right collector." He put the book on the counter before blowing off the dust. "I think Barker would see value in this."

The dust travelled through the air to Sue, tickling her nose. She let out a loud sneeze, which echoed around the barn. She immediately stood up, her hands cupping her bump, the look on her face saying it all.

"I need to go," she whispered, her eyes wide and her cheeks red from embarrassment. "Oh, I *really* need to go."

She quickly kissed Julia on the cheek before hobbling out of the barn, half-hunched over. Julia chuckled to herself as their father watched on, clearly confused.

"Women's troubles," Julia whispered with a knowing nod. "What is it?"

"A very early rare edition of *The Moonstone* by Wilkie Collins," he said as he dusted down the ancient looking thick volume. "First published in 1886 in Charles Dickens' very own magazine before making its way into hardback, it's considered by many to be the first modern example of the murder mystery books we know today. Considering Barker's current pursuit into the world of fiction, I thought this was an appropriate gift."

"It's perfect," Julia whispered as she carefully pulled back the cover to peer at an illustration of three Victorian men and a woman stood around a table. "But I don't think I can afford this."

"I've seen these go for upwards of two thousand pounds at the right auctions," Brian said, crossing his arms as he leant against a cabinet of army medals behind him. "But for you, I'll let you have it for a hug for your old dad. And before you tell me you can't accept it, I've been clinging onto this book for months because I had a feeling you might come in here looking for something for Barker, so just accept it."

"Are you sure?" Julia asked, looking down at the

book as though it was as valuable as the crown jewels. "I think he will really appreciate it."

"Then that's all that matters!" he announced as he wrapped up the book in brown paper before securing it in string. "Now, about that hug?"

Julia walked around the counter to give her father a hug, but they were interrupted almost immediately by the vibrating of her phone in her handbag. She pulled it out, surprised to see Johnny Watson's picture flashing on the screen.

"I should take this," Julia said with an apologetic smile. "We'll resume the hug in a second." Julia accepted the call and pushed the phone against her ear as she walked away from the counter. "*Hello*? Johnny? Is everything okay?"

"Julia?" Johnny whispered down the phone. "Are you alone?"

"I'm with my dad," she whispered back, glancing over her shoulder to smile at Brian as he resumed looking at the medals. "Has something happened?"

"I don't want to tell you over the phone," Johnny whispered even quieter. "I was looking over the pictures I took on the opening night of the play. I think I've found something. Can we meet somewhere private?"

***

JULIA HURRIED THROUGH THE DARK village to her café. She waited in the kitchen for Johnny to knock on the back door. When he did, she almost jumped out of her skin before letting him in.

"I hope you weren't busy," Johnny said as he crept into the kitchen, glancing over his shoulder into the dark. "I felt like I was followed the whole way here."

"Were you?"

"Maybe I'm just being paranoid," he said, pulling his canvas messenger bag over his shoulder before taking out a cardboard file. "I thought about taking this straight to the police, but I wanted to give you a chance to look over it first."

Johnny fiddled with his glasses as he stared down at the file on the stainless-steel counter. Julia stared at it for a moment too before deciding it was ridiculous to treat whatever was inside like a ticking time bomb. She flipped open the file, a dozen glossy photographs stacked up inside.

"What have you found?" Julia asked as she stared at the top photograph, which appeared to be a picture of the stage at the village hall before the start of the opening show. "Put me out of my misery."

Johnny separated the photographs, all of them looking like variations of the same thing. Nothing immediately jumped out at Julia.

"I was looking over the pictures again to make sure I hadn't missed anything," Johnny said. "When I heard about Poppy, I thought I might find something connected to the new information. I took this picture quite early in the evening before anyone arrived. I knew I wasn't going to use it, but I wanted to get a feel of the space and the lighting so I could get the best shots when things started. I originally dismissed this picture because it didn't seem important, but when I knew I was looking out for Poppy, I saw this."

Johnny pointed to a vaguely red blur in the darkness next to the stage. Julia squinted, but she couldn't see anything of interest. As though reading her mind, Johnny moved her further down the row of pictures.

"I have a feature called '*burst*' on my camera," Johnny said. "It means it will start capturing images from the moment it senses my finger pressing down on the button, and after. It picks the middle shot as '*the shot*', but you can go into the burst to see the pictures around it. It's important when you're photographing action, just so you get the best shot every time."

"Okay?" Julia said, still not seeing anything other than a red blur in the darkness next to the stage. "I still don't see anything."

"These six pictures are from the burst," Johnny said, circling the first lot of pictures in the row. "When I saw the red, I looked at the burst to see if it *was* Poppy that I was seeing. It's dark and grainy, right? You can't see much."

"I need my eyes tested," Julia said, putting her face right up to the picture. "I'm putting it off."

"Well, take it from someone who wears glasses," Johnny said with a fiddle of his frames. "You can't really see much, which is why I opened up my editing software to play around with the levels. By this point, I wasn't expecting to find anything, I was just looking out of curiosity to see if it was Poppy, or if I was chasing a white rabbit down a hole."

Johnny moved Julia down to the second lot of photos, which depicted the same scene, just much brighter. Suddenly, the dark shadow next to the stage was much lighter, and Julia could see two figures in the first picture. Just from the red hair, she could see that the blur did belong to Poppy's vibrant hair.

"What does this prove?" Julia asked as she looked at the pictures. "I still don't see anything incriminating."

"How about if I do *this*?" Johnny picked up the edited pictures and stacked them on top of each other before flicking through them like a child's picture book. "See anything now?"

Julia watched as Poppy darted down and then up again, something in her hands. Johnny flicked the six pictures back and forth, and she watched her spring up and down until she felt like she was watching a grainy video clip.

"You still can't see much, can you?" Johnny said, reaching into his bag for a second file. "Stay with me. I needed to walk you through this, so you didn't think I was jumping to conclusions. My camera is quite high quality, so I was able to zoom right in on that area and sharpen everything up. It's not perfect, but tell me what you see."

Johnny pulled out a second stack of photographs and flicked through them. This time, Julia could see the headset on Poppy's head clearly, as well as the clothes she had been wearing that night. She watched as Poppy bent down and up again, something metallic in her hands. Julia squinted, her heart suddenly stopping when she realised what was happening between her and the second figure.

"They *dropped* the gun," Julia exclaimed, her hand drifting up to her mouth. "They dropped the gun and Poppy was just picking it up for them! *That's* how her fingerprint got on it. She probably thought it was the prop."

"So, you *do* see it," Johnny cried, his hand slapping down on the counter. "I'm not going crazy."

"But who is the other person?" Julia asked, squinting at the shadow, the only thing visible was a hand accepting something from Poppy with a cloth. "That could be anyone."

"It could," Johnny said, reaching into his bag to pull out a single glossy photograph. "But I took another picture about ten seconds later after adjusting my camera's white balance. Are you ready for this?"

Johnny slapped the picture on top of the others, this one needing no explanation whatsoever. The figure had stepped out of the shadows and into the bright lights of the village hall, and was walking away from Poppy, who was heading further backstage none the wiser about what she had just done. The figure was clearly clutching something heavy and solid in a stained cloth. Julia squinted at the object in the cloth, which could very easily be a gun, and then up at the face of the person holding it.

"Oh, Johnny," Julia whispered, her mouth suddenly dry as she stared at the figure holding the suspected gun. "You did fall down the rabbit hole, but you found Wonderland."

"Carlton Michaels," Johnny replied firmly, jabbing his finger on the old man's face. "The *cleaner* switched the guns."

CHAPTER 14

Julia hurried into her cottage closely followed by Johnny. The warming scent of beef stew and gravy hit her immediately, rumbling her stomach; she was hungry, but there was no time to eat.

"Why is your window boarded up?" Johnny asked as he closed the front door behind them.

"Long story," Julia said. "Just wait here for a

second."

Keeping on her shoes and coat, Julia hurried down the hallway and into the dining room, where Barker was pouring white wine into two glasses at the neatly set dining table, a candle flickering between two empty bowls.

"*Ah!*" Barker said, turning around to kiss her on the cheek. "I was wondering what was holding you up. I thought we could have a date night indoors. Jessie is at Billy's, so I thought it would be the perfect opportunity to share some news with – *Oh*. Hello, Johnny."

Johnny stood in the dining room doorway, smiling sheepishly at the romantic setup, clearly knowing what he had walked in on.

"Barker, I'm so sorry," Julia whispered, resting a hand on his shoulder. "I didn't know you were planning this."

"It's okay," Barker said, glancing at a letter on the edge of the table. "It can wait. It's only my mum's slow-cooker beef stew, so it will stretch to three. Are you hungry, Johnny?"

Julia looked into Barker's eyes, wishing tonight of all nights was not the night she had to drag him out of the house to confront a cleaner who had slipped under the radar at every possible turn. She looked at the beautifully set table, and then at the letter; was that what he had been trying to talk to her about all week?

"'*Mystery Triangle Publishing*'?" Johnny remarked as he stared at the letter on the table. "Is it a rejection letter for your book? I've had three from them so far. It's almost impossible to get a publishing deal the traditional way these days, especially with those guys. It's all about online now. I heard about a woman whose cousin swears her friend's brother, or something, made –"

"Actually," Barker said, picking up the letter with a nervous smile. "It's *not* a rejection letter. I didn't want to tell you like this, Julia, but every time I try to tell you, something interrupts us, so you may as well hear it too, Johnny." Barker pulled the letter out of the envelope before passing it to Julia. "I started researching online about what I should do with my book when it was finished. I found a website for novice writers to find agents. I read on a forum that most places don't take unsolicited manuscripts these days, so I sent a sample out to a couple of agents. One of them, Max Byrne, had heard all about the murders in Peridale this year, and he thought the chapters he read were promising, and with some work, the book could really go somewhere."

Julia read over the letter, her heart skipping a beat when she saw the monetary value printed in bold letters halfway down the sheet.

"They've offered you a book deal?" Julia whispered, the letter trembling in her hands. "With a ten-thousand-pound advance?"

"It turns out, the publishers *really* liked the book," Barker said with a strained laugh. "The second Max told them about the real-life connection, they bit his hand off. This letter came last week."

"But I thought you hadn't even finished it?" Julia replied, looking at the typewriter in the corner. "You're always in here writing."

"I've already started on the sequel," Barker admitted, his eyes wide like a child confessing something naughty to his mother. "Read at the bottom. They've offered me an upfront *three*-book deal with an option for more, and bigger advances based on the success of the first book. They're looking to publish early next year. It's all happened so fast, it doesn't quite feel real. I didn't want to tell you I'd finished the book because I knew you'd want to read it, and I was nervous about what you'd think, mainly because you're in it, and I value your opinion above any of these people."

"You've been offered a *three-book* publishing deal?" Johnny mumbled, his eyes vacant as he stared at the flickering candle. "*Unbelievable*. That's my dream."

Julia read over the letter again, completely lost for words. She let the scale of the situation sink in, Marcus' murder and Johnny's photographic discovery suddenly meaningless.

"Please say something," Barker whispered with a nervous smile as he ran his finger down Julia's cheek. "Don't be mad at me."

"*Mad* at you?" Julia said, almost choking on the words. "Barker, I couldn't be prouder if I tried."

With the letter in her hand, Julia threw her arms around Barker's neck and squeezed him tightly, savouring the moment, knowing what had to come next. She stared at the typewriter in the corner, guilt consuming her for not thinking Barker's writing was going to go much further than Peridale.

"Beef stew?" Barker announced, clapping his hands together when Julia finally let go. "All this excitement has worked up an appetite."

Julia glanced over her shoulder at Johnny, who still looked dumbfounded at Barker's news, and then at Barker who seemed to finally realise that something was wrong, and that it was not usual for Julia to turn up late home from the café with Johnny Watson.

"We know who switched the guns," Julia said, nudging Johnny to produce the pictures from his bag. "And we need your help to trap them into a confession."

***

AFTER EXPLAINING EVERYTHING TO BARKER, they drove into the village. Once they were parked outside the church, they silently watched the village hall, the yellowy lights pouring through the windows in the double doors. Johnny reached deep into his bag, pulling out a pair of binoculars.

"What?" Johnny cried when he noticed Julia and Barker staring at them. "I'm a journalist. You never know when you're going to need to stake out."

"Have you ever used them before?" Julia asked as he pushed the binoculars up against his eyes.

"Well, no. But aren't you glad I have them now?"

While Johnny surveyed the village hall, Barker looked over the pictures again, shaking his head as though he didn't believe what he was looking at.

"It's a gun," Barker said as he looked at the picture of Carlton holding the cloth. "That much is for sure. It certainly explains how Poppy's fingerprint ended up on it."

"She was just being nice," Julia whispered as she looked around the dark village. "Is that Catherine?"

They all turned around in the tiny car to look where Julia was pointing. Dressed in a long black trench coat, Catherine walked past Julia's café and towards them, so consumed with looking over her shoulder that she did not notice the full car when she walked past. She slipped through the open church gates and hurried towards the village hall. Instead of walking through the front door, she danced around the side.

"What's she up to?" Barker whispered before looking down at the pictures again. "Are you sure you don't want me to call for back up, Julia? This all seems a little shifty."

"Not until I have a confession on *this*," she said, lifting up her phone. "For the sake of vindicating my gran, and Poppy, we *need* an airtight confession. You said it yourself. If we take this to the police, there's nothing guaranteeing that DS Christie will see what we see, and even if they arrest him, he could just say '*no comment*' during the interview. We need to catch him out."

"I still don't know what his motive is," Johnny thought aloud as he squinted through the binoculars. "Why would he *want* to kill Marcus? He's been working here for years."

"I don't know yet," Julia said as she looked down at the pictures in Barker's lap. "But I hope we'll find out soon."

"I see him!" Johnny exclaimed. "He's just come out of the cleaning cupboard with one of those huge industrial floor cleaning machines. Should we move?"

Before Julia could answer, a knock on her window made them all jump. Julia whipped around and squinted into the face of Ross, his clipboard still in his hands.

"What are you doing?" he asked after Julia rolled down her window. "Are you waiting for someone?"

"None of your business," Johnny said as he hid the binoculars in his jacket. "It's not illegal to sit in a car."

"I never said it was," Ross said with a chuckle. "In that case, I'll leave you alone. I've tried to let everyone know that tonight's performance was cancelled, but I have a feeling some people are still going to turn up, so I thought it would be best if I was here to explain the situation to people personally. Can't leave it up to Carlton, can I?"

The faint yet distinct sound of smashing glass in the opposite direction made them all turn back to the village hall. They sat in silence for a minute before Julia remembered what had happened before Ross turned up.

"Catherine!" she cried as she jumped out of the car. "She just snuck around the back of the hall."

With Ross taking the lead, they trailed after him through the church gates, following the path Catherine had just taken. They reached the back of the hall, light flooding out of one of the windows overlooking the graveyard.

"That's *my* office," Ross groaned before he ran towards the smashed window.

They all huddled around the window, which had been cleared of its glass completely. With her back to them, Catherine was digging through one of the drawers in the desk, throwing papers everywhere as she looked for something.

"What are you doing?" Ross cried as he climbed through the empty window frame. "Are you looking for money?"

Catherine spun around, a fistful of paperwork in her hands. She let it flutter to the ground before taking a step back to the door behind her. Julia jumped through the frame, followed by Barker, and then Johnny.

"You're just missing Scooby Doo," Catherine snorted as her eyes drifted across the unlikely group before landing on Julia. "Why can't *you* just keep your nose out of other people's business? *Hmm*? I've heard *all* about you because people around this village have a *lot* to say. Regular little Miss Marple, aren't you?"

"What are you doing here, Catherine?" Ross cried as he looked at the mess she had made. "I thought you'd already be long gone by now."

"I'm looking for what I *deserve*," Catherine cried, taking another step towards the door. "I put six months into this. I'm not leaving here empty handed. I know you keep the ticket money in here somewhere, Ross. Be kind to your Auntie Catherine. Give me what I'm *owed*. I'll vanish before sunrise, and you'll never see me again."

Catherine and Ross stared at each other for what felt like a lifetime, bringing to mind a scene from an old Western movie. Julia waited for one of them to make the first move, and she was not surprised when Catherine darted around and launched herself at the door. She rattled the handle, but it did not shift.

"Do you really think I would leave my office unlocked?" Ross cried as he dropped his clipboard onto his cluttered desk. "Not only are you a terrible actress, but you're also as dumb as a rock. I'm not giving you a penny, and now you've got yourself caught in the middle of a breaking and entering, and an attempted theft charge with four witnesses."

Like a deer caught in the headlights, Catherine stared wide-eyed at them before she darted to the window. Julia admired her attempted dash for the window, but she landed straight in Barker's arms, who restrained her in seconds. He unclipped a pair of handcuffs from the back of his belt before cuffing her hands around a thick pipe on the wall.

"You never know when you're going to need to handcuff someone," Barker said with a shrug when he noticed Julia and Johnny staring at him. "I wasn't walking into a stakeout unprepared."

"And you laughed at my binoculars," Johnny mumbled with a roll of his eyes. "What now? Do we call the police?"

"Not yet," Julia said with a shake of her head. "We need to finish this. Barker, do you have those pictures?"

He reached into his back pocket and pulled out the rolled up glossy pictures. Julia unravelled them and looked at the picture of Carlton holding the cloth-covered object.

"Someone needs to stay here and watch Catherine," Julia said, turning to Barker and Johnny. "Rock, paper, scissors?"

"Johnny can stay here," Barker said firmly. "I'm not leaving your side. You've walked into danger too many times without me."

"Danger?" Ross asked as he started to gather up the mess Catherine had made. "Why don't you tell me why you were really sitting outside in your car?"

"We've found something that will end this once and for all," Julia said, tapping the photographs. "Can you unlock the door? I need to talk to Carlton."

Ross stared at them suspiciously for a moment before doing as she asked. Julia hurried through into the backstage area, stuffing the photographs into her handbag next to the thick paper-wrapped book from the antique barn. With Barker on her heels, they hurried around the back of the stage towards the rumble of the floor buffer. When they passed Dot's dressing table, Julia felt the importance of the situation suddenly bear down on her.

"Let me do the talking," Julia whispered as she turned on the voice recorder on her phone. "And shut that floor cleaner off. I need to hear him talk."

"Just be careful," Barker replied as they slipped out of the dark backstage area and into the brightly lit hall, passing the exact spot in Johnny's pictures. "We don't know what he's capable of."

Leaving Barker behind, Julia approached Carlton slowly, his back to her. Under the bright lights, his bald head shone brightly, and he looked weak and frail as he pushed the huge machine across the floor, bringing it up to a brilliant shine. When she got close, she could hear him mumbling under his breath.

"Carlton?" Julia called out over the sound of the machine. "Carlton? Can I talk to you about something?"

The cleaner barely looked up at Julia before spinning around to head in a different direction, mumbling all the way. Julia followed him and called out again, but the old man changed direction once more. Julia nodded to Barker, who was standing by the plug sockets next to the cleaning storeroom. He yanked on the cable, the machine cutting off immediately.

"I'm not *finished*!" Carlton cried, his eyes looking down at the shiny floor. "So many footprints. Why are you making more footprints?"

"Carlton, I need to talk to you about the opening night of the play," Julia said, her voice shaking as she tried to make eye contact with the man who seemed adamant about looking anywhere else. "About Marcus' shooting."

"Blood stains are hard to get rid of, you know," he mumbled, his finger tapping on his chin. "Took strong bleach to bring it up out of the wood. I've been here long enough to have seen every stain you can imagine. Always stains and footprints in my hall. People never learn. I should have retired when I had the chance."

Julia looked at Barker, unsure if they had got the wrong end of the stick entirely. As she stared down at the old man, who was still grumbling under his breath, she wondered if he was capable of planning out a murder.

"Is there anything you want to tell me about the shooting?" Julia asked, all of the questions she wanted to ask drifting out of her mind. "About the gun switching?"

"I never got what I was promised," he grumbled before suddenly turning to walk back to his cupboard. "Still here cleaning up footprints."

Carlton shuffled into his cleaning storeroom. He pulled out a smaller manual floor buffer and started to work on the footprints Julia had caused.

"Carlton," Julia said, grabbing his shoulders and ducking down so that they were finally making eye contact. "I know you switched the guns. I have proof."

"Never knew it was real," he mumbled before shuffling off. "Never told me."

"What is he talking about?" Barker whispered, his brows arched. "He's crazy."

Julia opened her handbag, moved the book out of the way, and pulled out the photographs to show to Carlton. Something stuck to the pictures before fluttering to the ground. It was the slip of paper Ross had given to her to pass onto Dot in the shoe shop, his name '*ROSS MILLER*' spelled out in giant capital letters above his phone number. With shaky hands, Julia pulled her phone out of her bag. She exited out of the voice recording app and opened up her photo album, which was still open on the most recent picture she had taken. She scooped up the slip of paper, holding it next to the picture of her name.

"The letters are the same," Julia whispered, her hands shaking. "'*STAY AWAY. OR YOU'LL BE NEXT*'. Barker, look at this. It's the *same* handwriting."

Julia passed her phone and the slip of paper to

Barker before turning to watch Carlton shuffle off with the floor buffer. As all of the pieces of the puzzle slotted neatly into place, she suddenly realised just how wrong she had got everything.

CHAPTER 15

L eaving Barker in the hall, Julia sprinted back to Ross' office. She rattled the handle, but he had locked the door once again.

"*Ross?*" Julia cried as she banged her fist on the door. "Ross? Are you in there?"

Ross did not call back, but she heard muffled screams that she knew belonged to Catherine. Julia looked at the door, and then around her for something to break through with. When a red fire extinguisher caught her attention, she immediately picked it up and began bashing at the handle.

"What have you figured out?" Barker cried as he ran backstage. "I thought Carlton switched the guns?"

"He did," Julia yelled as she beat the extinguisher down on the handle one final time before it sprang off. "But didn't you hear Carlton? '*I didn't get what I was promised*'. This is what it's all been about since the beginning."

"What?" Barker replied.

"Money."

Julia burst through the door and fell into the office. Johnny was on the floor, blood trickling from the side of his head, his glasses snapped next to him. Catherine was still bound to the pipe, but a tie had been stuffed in her mouth, gagging her screams.

"He took the money and ran," Catherine cried when Julia pulled down the gag. "The guy with the glasses wouldn't move, so Ross hit him with the safe box."

Julia rushed to Johnny's side, relief spreading through her when she heard him groan. His eyelids fluttered, but he did not seem fully conscious or aware of what was going on.

"Stay with him, Barker," Julia called over her shoulder. "I need to go after Ross before he gets away."

Without waiting for him to object, Julia launched through the broken window, landing on the grass with a thud. She looked around in every direction, wondering which way to run, but when she heard the unmistakable roar of her car's vintage engine, she set off sprinting towards the front of the church, cursing herself under her breath for having left her keys in the ignition.

Julia jumped over the low church wall, landing in front of her car at the same moment Ross figured out how to turn the headlights on. They locked eyes as he revved the engine, his desperation to get away loud and clear.

"I *will* run you over," Ross cried over the roar of the car. "*Move!*"

"*No!*" Julia cried back, planting her hands on the car bonnet. "Not until you tell me why you planned to use my gran to kill your uncle."

Ross' nostrils flared as he revved the engine again. He edged forward, causing Julia to jump back, but she did not move out of the way. Ross looked through the rear-view mirror at the car parked behind him, and then at the village green.

Julia knew exactly what he was thinking, and if she let him get away, she doubted she would see him or her car ever again.

"I *warned* you!" he yelled before stamping his foot down on the accelerator. "You just couldn't keep out of things!"

The wheels spun, screeching against the fresh, soft snow. The headlights burning her eyes, Julia saw her life flash before her in an instant. She thought about Barker's book deal and how she would never get to see his success, and about how she would never see the day that Jessie was legally her daughter, or her sister's twins' birth, or her gran's freedom. She even thought about her mother resting a stone's throw away in the graveyard and how she would not get to lay flowers on her grave on Christmas morning.

Julia clenched her eyes, but the car never hit. Something as heavy as a car banged into her side, pushing her clean out of the way. She fell with a thud on the road, rolling onto the village green just as the front of her beloved car hit Barker.

"*No!*" Julia cried out as she watched him roll across the road.

Ross swerved out of the way, quickly losing control of the wheel. He mounted the pavement with a thud, crashing into the church wall with a crunch. Julia did not care about her car or about Ross' guilt, all she cared about in that moment was Barker. She ran over to his side, her own pain from hitting the road vanishing. She rolled him over, relief surging through her when she saw his clenched-up face.

"I'm fine," Barker mumbled through tight lips. "He barely touched me. Help me up."

Using Julia as a crutch, Barker stumbled to his feet. They both turned to her car as Ross stumbled out, dazed from the ordeal. He staggered down the street, the ticket money safe box clenched to his chest. When he finally seemed to regain his wits, Johnny climbed over the wall right in front of him, his fist colliding with Ross' right cheek. Johnny jumped back and yelped in pain as he clenched his hand, but Ross fell onto the snow, knocked out cold.

"I didn't see that," Barker said, nodding at Johnny. "He *tripped* over. Help me get him back into the hall. We're putting an end to this *right* now."

***

JULIA PACED BACK AND FORTH IN FRONT of Ross, who was tied up in the middle of the village hall with the long electrical cord from the floor buffer. It took him almost ten minutes to fully come to his senses, but when he started to wriggle against his restraints, Julia had lined up all of the details in her mind. When she was ready, she nodded to Johnny, who was recording the whole thing on Julia's phone, a bandage from the first aid kit strapped around his head. Barker was slumped over a chair, an ice pack on his knee, while Catherine and Carlton watched from the sides.

"You've lost the damn plot, woman!" Ross cried as he thrashed in the chair. "You can't do this to me!"

"The plot," Julia said. "That's where all of this started, wasn't it, Ross? I suppose you had the idea to stage this elaborate cover-up the moment your uncle, the only living relative that you knew you had, told you about the drama club. What did you tell me? That you bumped into each other in a bar a couple of months ago and you came to Peridale to overhaul the drama club? Did he also tell you about his cancer then as well? I bet you were already spending your inheritance from that moment, until you heard about his new wife."

"You can't prove a damn thing!" Ross yelled through gritted teeth. "This is just a story."

"A story," Julia echoed. "You wrote and directed

the play. '*A Festive Murder*'. It was billed as a murder mystery set at Christmas, and yet there was no mystery. We all saw my gran shoot and kill your uncle, which is exactly what you planned. You wrote the play especially for them, and I bet you were rubbing your hands together when my gran told you about their history. You told her to use it, but it was you who used it. And yet, when I asked you about it, you claimed not to have known their history. I should have caught you out then. You knew it would be a reasonable motive to keep the police off your scent until you finished your shows, leaving you to flee with your uncle's money the moment the dust settled. But that's not how it all worked out, is it? I suspect you'd have been happy to watch your uncle die of cancer, so you could cash in your inheritance. You were, after all, his only living relative. I suppose he made no secret that he was leaving his fortune to you? When you met Catherine, you were threatened. You told me yourself that you thought she was only in it for the money."

"She was," Ross said, spitting on the ground. "She's an opportunist."

"You don't know the half of it," Johnny mumbled under his breath as he cast his eyes at

Catherine, who was suddenly interested in her chipped nail polish.

"You thought the money was owed to you," Julia continued. "You probably still do. You didn't want to risk your uncle changing his will before he died, so you planned the play around killing him in such an obvious way that no one would suspect you because the whole village saw my gran perform your dirty work without any idea of what she was doing."

"So, why were Poppy's fingerprints found on the gun?" Ross asked smugly. "Answer that, Julia."

Julia unclipped her handbag to pull out the photographs once again. She held up the edited versions in front of Ross, flicking between them just as Johnny had for her.

"I imagine you were quite surprised to hear about Poppy's arrest," Julia said as she held up the picture of Carlton holding the cloth covered gun. "Especially since you put the cleaner up to switching the guns. You didn't want to risk any of this coming back to you, so you asked Carlton to do it. I bet you didn't even tell him it was a real gun."

"But he accepted the offer of money to not ask questions," Ross countered with a smirk, his eyes locked on Julia's. "He knew exactly what he was doing. My uncle's life was only worth five thousand pounds to him, but I suppose that's what happens when you've been scrubbing floors a decade past retirement age."

Julia looked at Carlton as he mumbled to himself, his fingers knotting together in his lap.

"You told me your grandfather, Marcus' father, was in the army," Julia said, suddenly remembering the small detail. "Is that where you got the gun? Was it left over from the war?"

"It was an Enfield No. 2," Barker announced. "Common army issue from the Second World War."

"That makes sense," Julia agreed with a nod as she continued to pace. "So, you already had the gun, you devised the story around killing your uncle, you made sure to use someone else to switch the guns so you were just an innocent bystander. You even played the part of the disgruntled director, sticking around and recasting the roles. The show must go on, after all, but the only show you were performing was saving face until your uncle's will was read. I bet you were happy when Catherine moved it forward."

"I wanted to see the look of disappointment on her face," Ross whispered darkly.

"And you did," Julia said with a nod. "Although you should have had a mirror on hand to see your own disappointment. I bet you were quite surprised to hear that Poppy Johnston had inherited every last penny."

Ross fidgeted in his chair, his eyelids fluttering for a second as he stared at Julia.

"I never did quite figure out that part," Ross admitted. "Indulge me. You seem to have everything else figured out."

"Poppy is your cousin," Julia whispered as she leaned into Ross' face. "Your uncle had a child he never even knew about until two weeks ago."

"That *witch*!" Catherine cried. "*That's* how she did it!"

"She didn't *do* anything," Julia said, her voice booming around the hall. "She wasn't like the nephew so desperate to inherit that he resorted to murder, or the wife who was waiting for the cancer to take over, so she could move onto her next victim. Poor Poppy was the only person in Marcus' life who actually cared. Given time to get over the shock, I daresay they would have enjoyed quality months before his death. Months you took away from her, Ross. Your own selfish need for wealth denied a confused girl the chance to get to know the father she had spent her entire life wondering about. In those two weeks, your uncle was clever enough to recognise that she mattered and that he cared about her, even if she was pushing him away. I wouldn't be surprised if you were only a few days too late after he changed his will."

"I checked," Johnny announced. "He changed it two days before the performance."

Ross glared up at Julia before thrashing against the cables once more. The news that he had missed out on his uncle's fortune by two days ignited fresh rage within him. Julia nodded at Johnny to move in closer with the camera.

"Have you got anything to say to my gran?" Julia asked. "The woman you happily framed for murder? Or what about the girl whose father you took away?"

"I'd do it all again!" Ross cried, his face turning bright red as he fought the restraints. "If it meant I had a chance at getting that money, I'd switch those guns again in a *heartbeat*!"

"Then that's all I need to hear," Julia said, nodding to Johnny to let him know he could stop filming. "Barker, you can call for back up now. We've got it."

Julia turned on her heels and headed for the door, satisfied with what she had heard. She glanced at Carlton, and she pitied the man whose simple mistake was going to see him joining Ross behind bars for his final years.

"How did you figure it out?" Ross called after her. "Tell me! I planned it so perfectly."

"Your handwriting," Julia said over her shoulder. "Your pathetic attempt at frightening me with a brick through my window was the tiny piece of thread I needed to unravel everything. When I compared it to the note you gave me to pass onto my gran, which I gather was all part of your performance, it became obvious they were written by the same person. I realised you'd told me everything else yourself, I just needed to put it under the right spotlight to see it clearly."

Ross let out a primal scream as Julia pushed through the double doors followed by Barker. Police cars sped from the station towards the village hall in seconds, the blaring of their sirens signalling a relief that everything was finally coming to an end.

"Your mind is brilliant," Barker whispered after he pulled Julia into his chest. "You've just given me even more material for my sequel."

"I'm glad to be of service," Julia said with a smile as the police officers rushed past them and into the hall. "Where do you think we can get a turkey from at this short notice? Gran will ask to stay in prison if we don't have a full Christmas dinner with all the trimmings."

CHAPTER 16

Julia walked alone into the quiet village on Christmas morning with a bouquet of yellow chrysanthemums. She walked past her gran's cottage, glad to see the curtains had been drawn, letting her know that Dot had returned home late on Christmas Eve as planned. She was itching to see her, but she was obeying her gran's request to be left alone until everyone descended on her house for Christmas dinner in a couple of hours; she imagined she had wanted the evening to get used to being back in her usual surroundings again.

Cutting across the snow-covered village green, Julia walked towards St. Peter's Church, avoiding looking in the direction of the village hall, which had been locked up since Ross and Carlton's arrests. After the eventfulness of the past two weeks, Julia was eager to enjoy the day of festivities and regain as much normalcy as possible.

After walking around the church, the snow crunching under her feet, Julia made her way to the other side of the graveyard to the peaceful spot under a giant yew tree where her mother had been laid to rest. When the tree came into view, she was surprised to see a wrapped-up figure already at the grave.

"You too?" her dad said through a smile after pulling down the black scarf covering his mouth. "Chrysanthemums. Your mum loved those at this time of year."

Julia laid the yellow flowers next to the pink bouquet of the same flowers her father had laid. Cuddled into her father's side, they stared down at the grave for what felt like a lifetime. She was thinking about everything and nothing all at once, her eyes glued to the faded picture of her mother behind a glass panel in the stone.

"She'd be so proud of you," he whispered as he rubbed her arm. "I hope you know that. Not just because you're living your dream with your café, but because of the amazing person you've grown into. What you've done with Jessie, and what you did for your gran shows what a remarkable woman you truly are, Julia."

Julia allowed a single tear to run down her cold cheek, only wiping it away when it reached her chin. She looked up at her dad, who seemed to have allowed more than one tear to streak down his lined face. Julia wiped them away with her scarf before tiptoeing up to kiss him on the cheek. They both turned at the same time as Sue hobbled towards them bump first with a bouquet of orange chrysanthemums. After laying her flowers, she cuddled into the other side of their father, and they stayed there as a family until they could not stand the cold anymore. In all of the years Julia had been visiting her mother's grave on Christmas morning, it struck her that this was the first one they had all been there together.

With promises to see each other for lunch later

at Dot's, they parted ways. Julia hung back near her café, watching her gran's cottage from a distance, the knowledge that she was inside offering comfort. When Dot threw her bedroom curtains back, Julia could not help but run across the green to her.

The front door opened to reveal her gran, out of her grey prison uniform and back in her pleated navy calf-length skirt, stiff blouse with a festive red brooch at the collar, and tanned tights with sensible shoes; it was easy to pretend she had been hiding away in her cottage since the opening night of the play.

"Oh, *Julia*!" Dot cried as they hugged in the hallway. "You have no idea how happy I am to see you. How long was I away? Weeks? *Months*?"

"Eleven days, Gran," Julia whispered as she clung to her, holding back the tears. "And you're never leaving again."

"Well, I might end up back there after my trial," Dot announced as she pulled away from the hug, already adjusting her brooch in the way she always did. "Thanks to the taped confession you got, they reduced my charges from murder to unintentional manslaughter, hence my sudden bail. Apparently, I'm no longer a danger to society, so I can walk the streets as a free woman. Considering the brilliant evidence you gathered, my lawyer thinks no jury on planet Earth would find me guilty of anything, but we'll have to wait until next year for my trial. You'd think I was Annie Oakley the way the people were carrying on! The girls back at the prison called me Dangerous Dot."

"You got a nickname in eleven days?"

"Oh, yes, dear," Dot said with a proud nod. "I was practically *running* the place! Say what you want about those girls, but they respect their elders, and I was the oldest con in there. It was nice for a holiday at Her Majesty's pleasure, but I'd much rather be here with my home comforts. There's only so many times you can eat lumpy mashed potatoes and indistinguishable mystery meat stew before one bores of it. I practically ate everything in my cupboards last night! I'd never been happier to see a chocolate digestive in my life, so I inhaled the whole packet in seconds. I don't know what we're going to eat for Christmas dinner. My cupboards are *bare*!"

"Don't worry about that," Julia reassured her. "Katie and Dad are bringing the turkey, Sue's bringing the vegetables, and I'm sorting out the desserts. It's all organised."

"You're a good girl, Julia." Dot cupped Julia's cheek in her palm with a soft smile. "Let's go for a walk. There's something I need to show you."

After Dot pulled on her winter duffel coat and scarf, she walked Julia beyond St. Peter's Church and the primary school, taking her deep into the frosty countryside. When they arrived at a vast empty field, they climbed over the gate and towards a large oak tree. Dot rested her back against the tree before taking ten paces towards another tree, and then three to the left. They stood side by side looking out at the beautiful view surrounding them, which was extra special in the winter months.

"We're currently stood on my square metre of land," Dot announced as she tucked her hands into her pockets. "This is what Marcus Miller sold me. Not worth killing a man over, but there's not much I can do with it. I sometimes come out here and just stand here like the queen of my castle. Maybe I should plant a tree in Marcus' honour?"

"That's big of you."

"I killed a man, Julia," Dot said, her expression dropping as she looked down at the frozen mud. "Regardless of what happened, I shot a man dead, and I will have to live with that for the rest of my life. Part of me feels like I should still be behind those bars, and if it wasn't for Ross' evil plan, I might have refused to leave. I took a poor girl's father from her before she got to know him. How is Poppy?"

"I went for lunch with her yesterday," Julia said as she looped her arm through Dot's. "She's still shaken up, but she's optimistic. She's spoken to a financial adviser, and even I was surprised to hear how much she had inherited. Half a million pounds in cash, and over a million pounds worth of prime London property."

"It's just money," Dot said with a shrug. "There are too many people with too many greedy thoughts out there."

"At least Poppy isn't one of them," Julia said as they set off back to the gate. "She said she's going to buy her mum a house, and she'll run the property business side of things while Poppy and Jayesh take a gap year to travel the world. They're starting in India to stay with some of Shilpa's family, and then the world is their oyster."

"Ah, to be young and full of hope again," Dot announced as she inhaled the crisp air. "Although, I suppose I've proved it's never too late. My acting debut might not have worked out, but I think I might get myself an agent and see if there are any jobs for any old gals like me out there."

"That's a great idea," Julia replied. "Out of all

the lies Ross told, I believed him when he said he thought you were a great actress."

"I suppose that counts for something," Dot said after climbing over the fence and holding out her hand for Julia to do the same. "Let's get back to the village. The table isn't going to set itself."

***

AFTER A LUNCH OF PERFECTLY COOKED turkey, honey-roast parsnips, roast potatoes, cauliflower cheese, chestnut stuffing, pigs in blankets, and cranberry sauce, the whole family moved into Dot's tiny sitting room, paper hats on their heads from the crackers. Katie and Brian took up the couch, with Vincent in his wheelchair next to them, and baby Vinnie on Katie's knee in his Christmas pudding outfit. Sue took the armchair, a mug of hot chocolate balanced on her bump with Neil on the chair arm, his hand also on the bump. Julia, Jessie, and Barker dragged in chairs from the dining room and sat where they could fit. Dot floated from person to person, offering drink top-ups, mince pies, and chocolates from one of many boxes that had been brought along.

"I'm stuffed," Brian announced as he

unbuttoned the top of his trousers. "Better than the muck the caterers would have made at the manor."

"I think we pulled together the best Christmas dinner in the whole of the country," Barker said as he also unbuttoned the top of his trousers. "Although, I don't think I can eat another bite until it comes around again."

"You're all weak," Jessie mumbled through a mouthful of mince pie. "I'm still hungry."

With Christmas music playing in the background they began exchanging presents. Jessie bought Julia a cookbook of unusual cakes from around the world, Brian and Katie gave her an antique brass and copper set of weighing scales from the late 1800s, Sue and Neil gave her a guide to the best cafés and tearooms in the Cotswolds along with a gift voucher for each, and Dot who had not had time to do any Christmas shopping, gave her a hug and a promise to make it up to her next year. Jessie loved the two new pairs of Doc Martens, and Barker loved the vintage copy of *The Moonstone*, which he seemed to know all about.

After all the presents had been handed out, they all sat in front of the roaring fire in what Julia could only describe as a food coma. The only person who did not seem affected was Jessie, who was making her way through the leftover coconut chocolates in the bottom of one of the selection boxes. After almost fifteen minutes of groaning and wrapper rustling, Jessie suddenly bolted upright, the silver foil wrappers falling off her stomach and onto the couch. She stared at the small tree in the corner, her brows heavy over her eyes. She stared down her nose at Julia, and then at Barker.

"Barker, you didn't get Julia anything," Jessie said, making Sue jump, who had nodded off. "That's a bit rubbish, don't you think?"

Brian shifted in his seat, as did Katie. They shared a grin for a moment before they both attempted to disguise it behind a cough. Sue rubbed her eyes with one hand, another hand on her bump. Barker sat up straight, his cheeks burning bright red. Julia had been so glad to all be together, she had not noticed that Barker had not given her anything.

"Thanks for that, Jessie," Barker said with a sigh as he reached into his pocket. "I was going to wait until later to give Julia her present."

"Ew," Jessie cried. "That's gross. I hope you wait until I'm out."

"Not like *that*," Barker said, his cheeks burning even darker. "I suppose there's no time like the present, is there?"

Julia looked around the room at the puzzled faces, Brian and Katie the only two who seemed in on whatever Barker was waiting to give Julia. With something in his hand, Barker walked into the middle of the room and stood on the hearthrug in front of Julia. Just when she was about to ask him what he was doing, he dropped to one knee as he produced a small, burgundy velvet box.

"I think I'm going to faint," Dot mumbled as she stumbled into a cabinet, rattling the ornaments. "Jessie, *catch me*!"

Jessie jumped up and looped her arm around Dot, who seemed to be auditioning for her next role. Julia stared down at the small box, her heart in her throat. She stared into Barker's eyes, wanting to say something, but unable to summon a single sound. Time seemed to stop, and the moment stretched out for all eternity before he finally snapped open the box. Julia was surprised when she saw a large, milky pearl perched on top of a silver band.

"My mum's engagement ring," Julia whispered, her hand drifting up to her mouth. "Where did you get that?"

"I kept hold of it all these years," Brian said before Barker had the chance. "I was waiting for the *right* man to ask for your hand."

Julia stared down at the ring, sure she had not seen it since the day her mother died. She had always assumed she had been buried with it, so to see it over two decades later was something of a surprise, although its beauty was unmatched to even her own memories.

"Julia," Barker started, the shake obvious in his voice. "I love you. I think that much is obvious. We've been through things that most people wouldn't survive, but every obstacle has made us stronger, which is why I wanted to ask you if –"

"*Hold that thought!*" Sue cried out as she bolted up, the hot chocolate cup bouncing off her bump before shattering on the carpet. "I think I just had a contraction!"

Whatever had been happening before suddenly no longer mattered. Within seconds, Neil was bundling Sue into the car ready to take her to the hospital, despite Dot's insistence that they should wait for the next contraction to see if it was real or not. Standing outside the cottage, Julia had her hand clamped in Barker's. She did not want to let go, but when she turned to him, he smiled and nodded, letting her know she should go with her sister.

"Family first," he said before kissing her on the cheek. "To be continued, okay?"

"I love you," she whispered after kissing him on the lips. "I'll see you later."

With Sue in the front seat and Neil driving, Julia and Dot sat in the back, with Dot nervously munching her way through a tray of mince pies, which she claimed she had grabbed in a panic. By the time they arrived at the hospital, Sue's second contraction had kicked in, letting them all know how they were spending the rest of Christmas.

"But I'm *early*!" Sue yelled as Neil wheeled her through the hospital towards the maternity ward. "I'm three *bloody* weeks early!"

"*Twins*!" Neil cried back as he rushed down the corridor, practically taking a corner on two wheels, their overnight bag on his back, which he had put in the boot of the car '*just in case*'. "I read all about this. Women carrying twins rarely carry full term."

"Where's Julia?" Sue cried, craning her neck over her shoulder, her hair whipping in the wind. "I need my sister."

"I'm right here," Julia cried back as she struggled to keep up with Dot, their Christmas dinner barely digested. "Don't you worry."

Julia did not expect that she would spend her Christmas evening holding Sue's hand as she went through the biggest event of her life, but she would not have spent it anywhere else. For the second and third time that year, she witnessed the miracle of childbirth right before her eyes as her sister gave birth to two baby girls.

"Pearl," Sue muttered as Neil wiped her forehead with a cold cloth when the midwife put the first baby in her arms. "After Mum."

"That's beautiful," Dot said as she wiped tears from her eyes. "On her birthday, too. She's looking down on you."

When the midwife took baby Pearl away and replaced her with the second girl, Sue looked up at their gran with a weak smile.

"Dorothy," she said as she stroked her newborn's face as her tiny lungs cried the room down. "After her great-gran. Dottie, for short."

"I think I'm going to faint for real," Dot murmured as she grabbed the end of the bed. "*Nurse!*"

After Neil dabbed down Dot's forehead with the wet cloth, the midwife ushered Julia and her gran out of the room to give the new parents time to bond with Pearl and Dottie. They had barely collapsed into two seats in the corridor when the lift doors slid open. Jessie, Barker, Katie, and Brian hurried in amongst a bundle of pink balloons and pink flowers.

"How did you get those on Christmas day?" Dot cried as she fanned herself with a copy of *Cotswold Life* magazine. "You couldn't get a pint of milk back in my day."

"I know a man who knows a chicken," Brian said as he hurried to the window, his heart seeming to melt the second he noticed his two granddaughters. "They're perfect."

While Brian and Katie met Pearl and Dottie, Jessie and Barker disappeared before bringing back polystyrene cups of tea.

"What time is it?" Dot asked as she let out a yawn. "I feel like I'm the in the Twilight Zone in here."

"Almost midnight," Jessie said after checking her phone as she sat next to Julia. "Christmas is almost over."

"Which is why I want to do this," Barker said, dropping to one knee once more with the pearl ring. "Julia, if I don't do this now, I'll regret it for the rest of my life. I want to marry you. I want us to be bound for the rest of our lives. I never believed in soul mates before I met you but –"

"Yes, Barker," Julia said, dropping down to kiss him. "I'll marry you."

She rested her forehead against Barker's, never surer of anything in her life. Barker picked up her left hand and slid the ring onto her finger; it fit as though it was made for her hand.

"Thank God you said yes," he whispered with a chuckle. "I don't think my knees could take dropping down for a third time."

They helped each other up off the ground, the ring feeling perfect on Julia's hand. With Barker's arm around her shoulder, she looked down at Jessie, who looked like she was attempting to smile, but could not quite muster it.

"Congrats," she mumbled. "I'm happy for you both."

"Just us?" Barker replied as he dragged her up to her feet to pull her into the hug. "I spoke to your social worker, Kim. She wasn't too happy to hear that I wanted to get married, but when I asked her if I could jump in on the adoption, she didn't think there would be a problem, especially now that Dot is out on bail. I want us to be a family, Jessie. I couldn't imagine a life without your eye rolls and teenage tantrums. Even if Julia and I are here one day like Sue and Neil, you'll still always be important to me – to *us*. Of course, only if you want that too. You *can* say no."

"Shut up, Barker," Jessie whispered before burying her face in his chest. "I don't want anything else."

Julia chuckled as she wrapped her arms around both of them. She was sure she heard Jessie sniffling into Barker's shirt, but neither of them said anything.

"Well, since you're all hugging, I might as well join in," Dot exclaimed before casting her arms around them. "And before you ask, I'm not crying, I'm just allergic to the cleaner they use on the floor."

Nothing had ever felt so right and perfect before in Julia's life, but as she looked over Barker's shoulder into the delivery room, her whole family around her, she could not imagine her life having taken her anywhere else.

"What a lovely end to a terrible month!" Dot exclaimed. "*Merry Christmas!*"

If you enjoyed *Gingerbread and Ghosts*, why not sign up to Agatha Frost's **free** newsletter at **AgathaFrost.com** to hear about brand new releases!

Don't forget to head over to **Amazon** to leave a review!

The 11th book in the Peridale Café series is coming early 2018! Julia and friends are back for another Peridale Cafe Mystery case in *Cupcakes and Casualties!*

11157582R00155

Printed in Great Britain
by Amazon